Celestial Desire

Abbie Zanders

Gary,
May all of your ever afters be happy ones :)
♡ *Abbie Zanders*

This is a work of fiction. Similarities to real people, places, or events are entirely coincidental.

Celestial Desire

First edition. August, 2015.

Copyright © 2015 Abbie Zanders.

Written by Abbie Zanders.

ISBN: 1517331706
ISBN-13: 978-1517331702

Acknowledgements

Cover design by the amazing Kim Killion of The Killion Group, Inc.

Professional editing by the incomparable M. E. Weglarz of megedits.com.

And special thanks to some very special ladies – Deb B., Anjee Z., Shelly S., Carol T., Tonya B., Susan J., Perryne D., Carla S., Stacy T., and Shayne R (and a few of you who prefer to remain unnamed – you know who you are) - for reading the first draft and making invaluable suggestions. This is a better story because of them!

… and THANK YOU to all of *you* for selecting this book – you didn't have to, but you did. Thanks ☺

Before You Begin

WARNING: Due to strong language and graphic scenes of a sexual nature, this book is intended for mature (21+) readers only.

If these things offend you, then this book is not for you.

If, however, you like your alphas a little rough around the edges and some serious heat in your romance, then by all means, read on...

Chapter 1

"Maybe we can have sex later."

Her eyebrows raised, and Zane felt the color flooding into his cheeks. "A *drink*," he corrected immediately. "I meant a *drink*. Maybe we can have a *drink* later." *Jesus, what was he, 15?*

The corner of that pretty mouth quirked and Zane felt the force of her gaze raking up and down his body from behind those dark, mirrored shades. Her head didn't move but based on the rolling, heated tingles licking over his skin, she'd checked him out head to toe at least twice in the few seconds it took her to respond.

"I'm not much of a drinker," she replied, and Zane almost shivered in pleasure at the sound of her voice. It was soft, muted. The kind of voice a man wanted to hear crying out in rhythmic, breathless gasps.

"Coffee, then. Do you like coffee?"

Another quirk from those soft, full lips, but she was no longer ogling him. Her eyes were looking directly into his now. It was impossible to tell what color they were behind the nearly-black lenses, but he had the impression that they were powerful, given the way his skin tingled when she looked at him. They probably sparkled, too.

"I like coffee."

Zane did a mental fist pump. He wasn't sure why he suddenly felt such a feeling of triumph; women rarely turned him down but there was something about this woman that was different. She wasn't the most beautiful woman he'd ever seen, or the best built; not even his usual type, really. Normally he went for the stereotypical California bleached blondes – tall, bronzed, lean and toned.

From what he'd seen so far, she was on the shorter side, a bit curvier than he was used to (what his grandfather would have called *voluptuous*), and she had light golden/brown hair the color of rich honey with streaks of sunlight. He couldn't put his finger on why he was so inexplicably drawn to her, which was just one more reason she warranted further study; so few women piqued his genuine interest beyond the usual 'she'll do'.

Out loud, he said, "That's good, because I like coffee, too. And afterwards, maybe we can -"

"Have sex?" she finished for him. The quirk had become a slow curving of her lips. The tingling intensified into a slow burn. When this woman smiled, it touched *all* of her features … and apparently some of his, too.

He rubbed the back of his neck, feeling more like an awkward teen than a twenty-seven year old Marine. He was almost afraid to look down for fear that he'd be sporting full-on wood, something no male ever wanted to happen while wearing jogging shorts, no matter what his age was. It was just that kind of day.

"If I'm lucky," he grinned sheepishly. He opted for boyish candor, instinctively sensing that smooth and slick – his usual M.O. - would not work on this woman.

"At least you're honest," she said thoughtfully, proving his theory.

"Some would say to a fault."

He received a full blown grin in response. *Yes!* She had a beautiful smile. It lit up her whole face and made it impossible not to smile in return.

"I'm Zane, by the way."

"Zane, huh? It fits you. I'm Celeste."

Celeste. Yes, he could see that. There was something very soft and fresh about her, and – dare he think it – her heavenly body. He groaned inwardly at the bad pun, glad that he'd at least had enough brain-to-mouth filters still engaged not to spew that little gem out there. He felt like he was hanging on by his fingertips here and one more *faux pas* would result in an epic fail.

After agreeing to meet at a trendy new coffee shop later that evening, Zane walked back to his place, the towel draped around his neck, feeling a lot better than a man who had just thoroughly embarrassed himself should. Fortunately, the pretty honeyed blonde didn't seem to take offense at his blatant Freudian slip, taking it all in stride with an unusually good humor rarely found in women these days. *And* she was going to join him for coffee later.

Maybe it was his lucky day after all.

* * *

From her chair beside the pool, Celeste watched the man walk away. The view from this angle was nearly as fine as the one from the front – a whole symphony of rippling muscles across his broad shoulders and back, tapering down into a lean, narrow waist that she now knew featured a six-pack on the other side. And his ass – it just might be the nicest one she'd ever seen on a man, blending perfectly into strong, muscular legs.

All of that was nice – really nice – but it was his roguish, youthful face that took her breath away. His eyes were the most amazing icy blue, surrounded by impossibly thick, dark lashes that were the same color as his hair – a rich, deep chestnut that captured the California sun and made it dance when he moved. His face was clean-shaven and looked baby-smooth but his lips were all grown-up. She probably shouldn't have stared at them as much as she had, but as with his eyes, they had commanded her instant and complete attention.

Celeste sighed. Now that he was out of sight, her internal temperature was starting to return to normal levels and her logical mind was entering

WTF mode. The last thing she needed was to become involved with someone. She'd moved into the gated community less than two days ago, and was hoping to stay long enough to fulfill her six-month condo lease.

The most womanly parts of her – the ones she'd neglected for far too long – reminded her that *Zane* probably wasn't interested in a long-term relationship. Maybe they could just hook-up, satisfy each other's curiosity, and be done with it. He certainly seemed like the type – gorgeous, sexy, a physique that gave women wet dreams, and playfully naughty. Definitely not the kind of man who would usually give her a second look, which made this possible opportunity even more tempting. Who knew when she might get another chance like this?

Celeste had never actually had casual sex before – her ex-husband was the only man she'd ever been intimate with – so she wasn't quite sure how it worked. Did they have to go out first? Should she expect him to pay, or should they go Dutch? Would they go back to his place or hers, or maybe seek neutral ground?

The whole idea was as terrifying as it was exciting, leagues away from her usual routine of remaining quietly in the background, watching everyone else have all the fun. Then again, she had moved out here to make a fresh start, hadn't she?

Celeste sat at the pool for a few minutes longer,

enjoying the peace and quiet of the beautiful morning. It was still early, barely seven a.m., but she liked the emptiness and solitude for her morning workout swim. Once others began to arrive, she pulled on her beach cover up, gathered her things, and slipped back to her new place to start her day with a spring in her step that hadn't been there before.

Chapter 2

"Damn." The coffee shop was temporarily closed for renovations. Zane had never been there himself, but he'd overheard enough people raving about it in and around their gated community to think it might be a good place to try. Cupping his hands against the glass, he peered in. It did look like a nice place – warm and cozy and the perfect place to break the ice, get to know someone a little before seducing them.

Yeah, he liked a bit of verbal foreplay before the main event; he wasn't a complete animal. Besides building the anticipation, it gave him a feel for what a particular woman might like. Some were wild and adventurous; others needed a gentler touch. Zane was flexible; he knew he'd be ending the evening on a happy note and liked ensuring his partner would, too.

"Hmm," she hummed beside him. "That's too bad. It looks like a nice place."

Zane looked down (she barely reached his shoulder), slightly surprised that she had spoken the same words that had been in his head only a second or two earlier. "Sorry about that."

Celeste tilted her head up, and he was stricken by her eyes. Fathoms-deep polished amber with swirls of mahogany looked back. She looked as disappointed as he felt. "It was a good idea. Another time, maybe."

He'd been looking forward to spending some time with her all day; there was no way he was going to let her get away from him that easily. "We could go somewhere else. Are you hungry?"

"No." She shook her head. "I wish I could say I was, but I ate just before I met you here." Zane wasn't hungry either; he'd done the same thing.

They stood there for a solid minute, neither wanting to part quite so soon before Celeste took a breath and said, "I've got a Keurig at my place."

Zane said a silent prayer of thanks that he knew what that was. His uncle had just gotten one, too.

"Yeah?"

"Yeah. If you're still interested in coffee, that is."

"I am."

Celeste gave him a shy smile that lit him up on the inside. Without thinking, Zane reached out and captured her hand, interlocking their fingers. It was only after he felt the warmth and tingles extending up into his arm that he realized what he had done. The last time he had held a girl's hand had been at the county fair in middle school, and *coffee* hadn't been involved.

As good as it felt, he rationalized that the move had just been his finely-honed instincts kicking in, adjusting to the situation. She seemed as surprised as he did, but she didn't pull away. In fact, after that initial hesitation, her fingers curled around his, perfecting the fit. Yes, Celeste was definitely the hand-holding type, and he was just being accommodating. His cock roused, agreeing whole-heartedly.

"Shall we?"

Her shy grin widened. "We shall."

"Just moved, huh?" Zane looked around the near-empty space. It was the same layout as his uncle's place, but seemed much bigger without anything in it. Except for a banquet-sized folding table holding what looked like various pieces of computer equipment and a rolling desk chair, the living space was bare.

"Yeah. Two days ago."

That explained why he hadn't seen her around before. "Computer geek? Or a fence dealing in stolen goods?"

"Definitely a geek," she laughed over her shoulder, just as he'd intended. Sexy *and* likable, a devastating combination, that. "I guess I should get some furniture at some point, huh?"

"Furniture is good." He watched as she filled the machine's reservoir with bottled water. Standing behind her as he was, he could appreciate her shapely legs, the way her skirt clung to the rounded curves of her ass. His perusal continued upward, visually tracing the curve that slid inward at her waist before it broadened again beneath the soft-looking, lightweight sweater.

Suddenly, Zane's interest in small-talk took a back seat to something much stronger.

* * *

Celeste turned around to find Zane right behind her, close enough to feel the scorching heat radiating from his body. She supposed she should have expected it; after all, she *had* invited him back to her place. To those well-versed in casual sex and meaningless hook-ups, the coffee invite was probably code for '*do me*', the one-cup capacity of the Keurig synonymous with a one-night stand. Her over-analytical brain wondered absently what it would have meant if she had an old-fashioned percolator instead, forcing her to suppress a nervous giggle.

He shifted slightly, only the tiniest ripple of muscle and mass, but the movement made her catch her breath. Part of her felt afraid and wanted to step away; a larger, more insistent part wanted to close the several-inch gap separating them to see if he was really as tightly packed together as he looked.

"Celeste." He whispered her name huskily

before his head lowered and he brushed the softest of kisses across her lips. She might have moaned softly; she couldn't be sure over the pounding of her heart or the roar of blood rushing through her veins.

Fear and excitement warred within her. Was she really going to do this? Could she suppress her natural inhibitions and have a meaningless fling based only upon carnal, physical pleasure? Granted, Zane was sexy and gorgeous and smelled amazing, and he certainly seemed like the kind of guy who would be very, very good at it, but...

Zane's large hand skimmed down her back and cupped her bottom, pulling her close against him. The feel of all that hot, hard, aroused male made it a no-brainer. She most definitely was going to do this, and she was going to enjoy every lubricous second of it.

* * *

Christ, that sound she made, he thought. He'd never heard a woman make a sound like that from such a chaste kiss; one breathless syllable that seemed to convey the same need and desire centered in his groin. He deepened the kiss; after only a moment's prodding, she softened and opened for him.

Time became irrelevant; he had no idea how long that kiss lasted. He was barely aware of the fact that he was holding her against the wall, keeping her softening body from sliding downward. Her hands burned like brands on his back, despite the cotton T that separated them from his bare skin.

He pressed his erection against her belly, wanting her to know exactly how interested he was.

"You're very aroused," she murmured.

He broke contact with her lips – now swollen and dark from his possession – and exhaled slowly, resting his forehead against hers as he struggled to calm his breathing. His hips, however, continued to roll in slight, sensual movements. "You're a very arousing woman."

He felt like a horny kid rubbing against her like that, but *damn*. Maybe he should try to cop a feel, too. His long fingers slipped under the hem of her skirt, tracing the skin along her outer thigh. Before he knew it, they were sliding beneath the silk of her panties, exploring. Discovering. He caught his breath about the same time she did.

"You're very wet."

Her eyes sparkled, just like he knew they would. "You're a very arousing man."

There was no reason to wait. Not when he was hard and aching and she was slick and ready. Before she could catch her breath, he stole it away entirely. One swift tug and the flimsy barrier of her delicate panties was history. He lifted her up against him; she instinctively wrapped her legs around his hips as he moved forward toward what he hoped was the bedroom.

"Are you on the pill? The ring? The rod? Get shots?"

"What?" she breathed. She looked up at him from the queen sized mattress occupying the far corner of the bedroom floor. Her expression was bemused, her eyes clouded with desire. He liked that look on her. A lot.

"Birth control," he clarified as he lifted her shirt over her head and buried his face in her substantial cleavage. With a skillful flick of his fingers, the front closure clicked open; he used his lips and teeth to peel apart the satiny, lace-trimmed cups as she arched beneath him, offering herself to him with a breathy plea of need. Zane reveled in the softness of her obviously natural breasts as his hands explored the slight, womanly swell of her abdomen. It had been a long time since he'd felt anything quite so real, quite so... arousing. His cock was like iron. "Are you on any kind of birth control?"

Another sound, this one deep and throaty as he sucked her hard nipple into his mouth, causing his shaft to throb insistently, demanding he move things along. It wanted inside this woman and it wanted her *now*. If the rest of him hadn't been in one-hundred percent agreement, the sheer intensity of his need might have given him pause.

"Um, no," she breathed apologetically. "It's... been a long time. Haven't needed to."

He knew it! This woman, as hot as she was,

was also incredibly inexperienced. Warning bells should have been ringing in his head, but they weren't. Or maybe they were and he just couldn't hear them over the pounding of his heart.

"Don't worry," he told her, pulling a foil packet from his pocket. "I've got this."

The relief in her eyes was tangible. She spoke volumes with those eyes. At the moment they were filled with longing and need, and something that he rarely saw in a woman's eyes in the throes of passion: amusement.

"Boy scout?" she teased.

Her amusement was not the turn-off it would have been under any other circumstance, because he recognized it for what it was - anxiety. She wanted him, but she was a little scared, too. He grinned back at her, hoping to alleviate some of her unease. If she changed her mind now, he'd probably experience the phenomenon of spontaneous combustion first-hand.

"How'd you know?"

"Always... prepared," she said, her eyes widening as she watched him sheath himself. "Um, Zane? I think we might have a problem."

Problem? No, there was no problem. There couldn't be. Not when he was so close to burying himself balls-deep in all that lush heavenliness. He would kill it, whatever it was. "What's that?"

"I don't think it's going to fit."

He grinned wickedly, using his finger to trace

around the outside of her sex, wondering at the amount of slick wetness she'd already spilled for him. "It will."

"But... how?"

"I'm very resourceful." He positioned himself over her, her stiff nipples and heavy breasts pressed against his chest. His hips fitted into the perfect cradle she created for him by widening her thighs and bending her knees; his thick, weeping head took the place of his finger, pressing teasingly at the tight opening. Even that little bit of pressure was enough to feel her stretching around him, desperate to accommodate him.

"Hmm," she hummed again. Pressed against her as he was, he realized that when she hummed like that her whole body vibrated. "Honest, prepared, and resourceful. Be still my beating heart."

She sucked in a breath as he slid the broad head just inside her entrance, stretching her to her limits. "Oh, my...."

As the first light of dawn began to peek through the blinds, Zane opened his eyes to find Celeste staring at him. Again.

"Stop looking at me like that," he commanded, his voice deep and husky. "I don't have any more condoms."

She traced lazy circles on his chest with her

fingers, regarding him hopefully from her perch atop his body. Eyes bright, naked and smooth, she was quite a vision, "I thought you were prepared."

He gave her a martyred look. "Three's usually enough."

"What can I say?" she smirked, wiggling her behind and making him groan. "I'm an overachiever."

He pulled her down to him, capturing her mouth in a hungry kiss. God help him, he wanted her again. By all reasoning, he shouldn't even be able to get it up but there he was, already sporting a semi and ready to go into a full-out salute with nothing more than a wiggle of that cute little ass. And he'd made her come no less than seven times over the course of the night. He knew. He was counting. He was a bit of an overachiever, too.

"Can I see you tonight?"

Hope flared in her eyes, then disappointment. "I can't. I've got a thing."

He was disappointed, too. He shouldn't be. He'd spent the last several hours tangled in the sheets atop the mattress (she didn't have an actual bed yet), wringing every last bit of pleasure from her lush little body. But he was. "A thing?"

"Yeah. I'm having dinner with my mom tonight."

For some reason, those words soothed him. It was strange. After all, he'd known her for what, less than twenty four hours? Why should he care if she was seeing someone else? This was just a hook-up, right?

Ignoring the strange feeling of relief, he folded his arms behind his head, mostly to keep from touching her. Her softness fascinated him; he couldn't seem to stop running his hands over all those curves and dips, squeezing and kneading, caressing and fondling every inch of her heavenly body. It was so much sexier than the lean, overly-toned bodies he was accustomed to. Far from being fat or even chubby, Celeste was the epitome of femininity. Lush. Soft.

"Tomorrow, then? Coffee?" he added with a wink.

She laughed, and he felt it spread through him like sunshine. "Maybe."

Maybe wasn't good enough. *Maybe* implied it might not happen, and that was unacceptable. Instead of his usual feeling of sated satisfaction, he was craving *more*. And if she kept wiggling her ass like that, he was going to break every safe-sex rule he had and bang her anyway. Just the thought of entering her bare, of coming inside her, had his balls swelling again.

"What can I do to sway you?" he said, glad that his voice didn't convey the desperation he felt.

Her eyes twinkled as she sat up and splayed her palms across his chest, appearing to consider it. "Bring more than three."

Lord, have mercy.

Chapter 3

"California agrees with you," Jessica Harrison commented. Mother and daughter sat at the small table for two in the quiet Italian restaurant, remarkably alike in appearance. Jessica's blonde hair now had a few silvery strands, and her face, a few more wrinkles, but rather than detract from her beauty, they added to it.

"This food agrees with me," Celeste said, eyeing up the perfectly prepared chicken medallions the waiter placed before her. The smell of lemon and herbs had her stomach cheering in anticipation. "Lean meats, fresh herbs and vegetables. Makes it easy to forget the carbs."

"You look wonderful, Celeste. I am so proud of you."

"Thanks, Mom. I feel good."

"Everything is okay? Do you need anything?"

"Everything is fine. Stop worrying."

"I'm your mother. Asking me not to worry is asking for the impossible."

Celeste reached out to touch her mother's hand. "But I'm okay. *Really*. I love my new place."

"I don't know why you just didn't move in with

me," Jessica said. "I have plenty of room."

"We've been through this, Mom." While Celeste loved her mother and wanted to be close to her, Jessica had a tendency to be a bit overprotective. It wasn't wholly without reason; the past two years had been difficult, but Celeste was stronger because of it. Not to mention she'd become accustomed to the freedom and privacy that came with living on her own. If she'd been staying with her mother, she wouldn't have experienced the wonder and magic of Zane, sex-god extraordinaire. That man had some *serious* skills.

"Yes, and you're right. But at least let me help. Let's go furniture shopping tomorrow."

Celeste hesitated, sipping from the tall glass of ice water. "Tomorrow?"

"Yes, tomorrow," her mother smiled. "There are quite a few good places around, and at least one of them is advertising a semi-annual sale. We can pick out a nice bedroom set, some chairs and tables, maybe a sofa."

"I don't need all that, Mom. My lease is only for six months."

Jessica's smile flickered. "I was hoping you might like it enough here to stick around a bit longer than that."

"I love it here. It's beautiful." Visions of a sexy, naked Zane flashed through her mind. "But I can't make a decision like that after only three days."

Jessica put down her fork and smoothed the napkin draped over her lap. "You're safe now, Celeste."

Celeste nodded, because she knew her mother wanted to believe that. Celeste wanted to believe it, too, but didn't have as much faith in the legal system as Jessica did, not where her ex-husband was concerned. She wanted to keep her options open and her life mobile enough to move on at the first sign of trouble. Coming here at all had been a risky move – Celeste did not want the shadows of her past darkening her mother's doorstep but figured it would be safe enough for the next few months, at least. And, truth be told, she'd really missed her mother and the close bond they had once shared.

"So what's Mitch doing this evening?" Bringing up her mother's special friend was a surefire way to lighten the mood and redirect the conversation to more pleasant topics. As hoped, Jessica's features softened and a smile played about her lips. It was nice to see; her mother's eyes hadn't lit up like that since her father died.

"He said he had some briefs to wade through before court tomorrow."

Mitch was a lawyer, and a good one. Celeste had met him on more than one occasion and heartily approved. "He is always welcome to join us, you know."

"I know, and I appreciate that, but we need

some mother-daughter time, too. Like dinner tonight. And furniture shopping tomorrow."

Celeste sighed. So much for her brilliant diversion tactic. "I'd love to, Mom, but I can't. I've got a ton of orders lined up, and the move put me behind."

"Business is good, then?"

"Better than good," she grinned. "I'll never have to work another day again." Jessica laughed at their inside joke, a reference to one of Celeste's favorite sayings: "If you love what you do, you'll never work a day in your life."

"I'm happy for you, honey. You deserve it. But surely you can spare an hour or two for your poor old mother?"

Celeste rolled her eyes at her mother's blatant attempt at guilt, but laughed. "All right! But only the kitchen store, no furniture."

"Deal. I need to pick up some things for the dinner party next week anyway."

The hairs on the back of Celeste's neck prickled in warning. "Dinner party? What dinner party?"

"Oh, didn't I tell you? I'm planning a small get-together, kind of a 'welcome to the neighborhood' thing."

"*Mom.*"

"What? It's just going to be a couple of people."

"You know I don't like those kind of things."

"You need to get out and meet people, honey. I promise, it won't be bad. Just some local business people who live in the complex. Potential local contacts. Please."

Celeste exhaled heavily. "I'll think about it, okay?"

Jessica smiled. They both knew Celeste would be attending. "Fine. Now about tomorrow. I was thinking we could start at …"

* * *

It was supposed to be a once and done thing; satisfy his craving, scratch his itch, then move on. Yet he found himself at Celeste's condo again two nights later. She'd called and like a slobbering hound he'd been out the door with the phone still held to his ear.

He hadn't been able to stop thinking about her, which should have bothered him more than it did. He rationalized it away, reasoning that because he'd underestimated her the last time, he needed to redeem himself before he could move on.

She was giving him a second chance, and he wasn't going to blow it. He tucked a dozen condoms into his pocket this time. Apparently she was just as anxious for a re-do, because her door flew open before he'd even lifted his hand to ring the bell.

Hungry eyes fixed on his and her pebbled

nipples were clearly visible beneath the white silk of her robe. He growled and stepped over the threshold, taking her in his arms while he kicked the door shut with his booted heel.

"Zane," she panted, "can you do that thing?"

"What thing?" his words were muffled against the soft skin of her neck, his breath coming as hard and fast as hers. Christ, he was like an animal around her! Within seconds of showing up at her door with a bouquet of flowers, she was naked in his arms and he was trying desperately to push his jeans down enough to free his aching erection.

"That *thing*," she pleaded, grinding her hips against him. At least he wasn't alone in this crazed lust. Less than forty-eight hours had passed since he'd walked out of her condo, but it might have been forty-eight weeks given the unbearable throbbing in his groin.

"You mean that thing where I shove my aching cock inside your tight wet pussy and fuck you till you scream my name?"

Her eyes rolled back in her head as he did just that. "Yeah," she exhaled in blessed relief. "*That*."

A week later, he was no closer to walking away. She was right out of his personal fantasy; sweet, smart, sexy as hell, and freaking insatiable. They'd make love and barely fifteen minutes would go by before he found himself lusting after her again. Granted, she had an incredible body, all soft, womanly curves, with generous natural breasts and hips that cradled his body and melded to every hard plane, welcoming him with heat and slick moisture. No matter how many times he prodded for entrance, she was always ready and willing.

Seven days since he'd first noticed her by the pool, and he'd seen her no less than three times. Those three times had consisted of marathon sessions in her condo, though they'd branched out a bit. They made heavy use of the mattress (she still didn't have a proper bed), but also explored the shower, the kitchen counter tops, and the section of wall just inside the doorway.

He touched the pads of his fingers to the raw-looking rug burn along her lower back, recalling how they had rolled off the mattress in their spirited play and he hadn't even thought about easing up. She winced at the slight contact; he made a mental note to put some ointment on that when he had the strength to stand again. The thought of her hurting was unacceptable.

"I was thinking of heading out to the marina tomorrow, doing some sailing. What do you say?"

"Sounds awesome, but I can't." Her voice was a soft purr as she stretched out languidly beside him.

"Another *thing*?"

"Yeah. I'm setting up a new system for someone." In between their bouts of epic sex, he'd learned that she designed, built, and installed custom computer systems. That explained all of the digital equipment piled in her living room when she didn't even have a decent chair to sit on.

"I thought you made your own hours."

"I do, mostly, but this isn't regular business."

"Postpone. Reschedule. Work your magic." He punctuated each word with a nip of his teeth, finishing with a couple of long, lingering licks.

She groaned and shifted, giving him better access while her fingers threaded through his hair to keep him from moving too far away. Celeste, it seemed, was every bit as greedy for his touch as he was for hers. "You make it hard to refuse, but this guy's really important."

"Guy? Should I be jealous?" His tone was teasing and light, but the unease in his gut was anything but.

"Relax," she chastised on the crest of another groan, arching her back as her breast bid for more attention. "You're more than enough man for me."

Feeling remarkably better, Zane started breathing again. "So who is he?"

"My mom's friend. She really likes him, and he's a great guy. He … did something for me. I'm hoping to repay the favor a little."

Zane didn't miss the way she averted her eyes; there was some undercurrent in her tone that had his protective instincts rushing to the surface. It was unsettling, to say the least. He'd known her what, a couple of days? He shouldn't be feeling this... territorial.

Then again, the normal rules didn't seem to apply when it came to Celeste. If she was anyone else he wouldn't have returned a third time. Once was usually his limit, twice if the sex had been truly epic. He wasn't sure he'd ever even made it to a third visit before, so he was in unfamiliar territory even when it came to rationalizing what it meant.

He shoved those thoughts to the back of his mind, unwilling to overanalyze while he had all this soft, warm flesh against him. Celeste and logical thought were proving to be nearly mutually exclusive.

"What did he do for you?" he pressed.

Her entire body tensed in his embrace. Was it in anger? Fear? Annoyance? Zane wished he could see her eyes so he'd have a better idea of what she was feeling; her every emotion was displayed clearly in them, he'd noticed.

He refused to let go when she tried to pull away. Instead, he let his hands move slowly over her back, soothing strokes meant to calm. After a span of several heartbeats, he felt her begin to soften again. He liked that he could have that kind of effect on her.

"You ask a lot of questions," she said finally against his chest.

"Add 'curious' to 'honest', 'prepared', and 'resourceful'."

She grinned slightly, but it faded as quickly as it had come. "It's a long story," she hedged. "Maybe another time, ok?" She pulled away from him, the first time she had done so. He didn't like it at all, but this time he allowed it.

"Okay," he agreed reluctantly. "But, Celeste?"

"Yeah?"

"I want to know more about you."

She gave him a sad smile and touched her fingers to his lips. She opened her mouth to say something, then changed her mind. Instead, she rose up on her toes and kissed the corner of his mouth. "Go on now," she said softly. "I've got work to do and you're too much of a distraction."

Zane wrapped his arms around her and pulled her close, giving her a proper kiss. If she thought he could be dismissed that easily, she was mistaken. But something was bothering her, and he had the feeling that if he pushed too hard she'd shut him down completely. That was the last thing he wanted.

"How about dinner, then?"

"Can't," she said. "Got a thing."

Another *thing*. He was fast becoming tired of *things* getting in the way of him trying to do something more than simply fuck her into ecstasy, and wasn't that a shocker? He shelved that little epiphany for later when he could examine it more closely. She was trying to move away from him again.

"You know, pretty soon I'm going to think you just want me for my rod."

She grinned, and the mischievous spark was back in her eyes. "Well, to be fair, it really is an amazing rod."

He heaved a martyred sigh, though his chest puffed out with male pride at the same time. If that's what it took to keep her around for a while, he'd man up.

"All right," she said, rolling her eyes. "Stop giving me those big puppy eyes. I can't do dinner, but maybe we can meet for dessert afterwards."

"*Puppy eyes*?" The Marine in him was mortified.

"Yes. You remind me of one of those Siberian huskies with the shocking blue eyes, damning and redeeming at the same time. It steals my breath away sometimes."

Well, hell. If he wasn't feeling that strange sudden tingle in his chest he might actually take offense. Then again, they were getting him what he wanted, so... "And coffee?" he asked hopefully, waggling his eyebrows.

"Definitely coffee," she laughed, tossing him his shirt.

With one or two more stolen kisses, Zane reluctantly left Celeste. It was probably a good thing she'd kicked his ass out; he had some work of his own to do.

He filled his lungs with the fresh, clean air; it

mixed with Celeste's subtle fragrance, intensifying that odd sensation in his chest again. Like it or not, his feelings for her were extending beyond the usual hook-up and surprisingly enough, he was okay with that. For the first time, Zane was the one wanting more, willing to see where things went.

The question was, was she?

Chapter 4

"What are you so happy about?" Mitch Fagan asked his nephew, glancing over the half-sized reading glasses he wore while reviewing his notes.

"Me?" Zane asked absently. He erased a few spots on the schematic he'd been working on, then made a few additional sketches.

"Yes, you. You're *whistling*."

"Am I?" Zane finally looked up from his drawings and met his uncle's eyes briefly. He gave him his best innocent look, but Mitch wasn't fooled for a minute. One of the reasons Mitch was such a highly successful attorney was because he had an innate ability to see through bullshit.

Mitch set down the papers and leaned back in his chair, crossing his muscled arms over his chest. He pinned his nephew with a meaningful look. The son of Mitch's identical twin, Zane was not only a younger version of him in appearance but in personality as well.

"You're scaring me."

Zane laughed. "It's cool, Uncle Mitch. I met someone."

"Did you now?" Mitch's voice softened in

cautious optimism. Zane was a good man, but he was restless. Ever since he'd come out to stay with him in the adult condo community, Zane had been going through one woman after another. He didn't need a psych degree to know that it was a defense mechanism, a way to keep people at arm's length.

He even understood the reasons *why* Zane was the way he was. In the past few years, he'd had to deal with the loss of people he'd cared about; first, some of his Marine brothers in a rescue op gone bad and then, when he'd completed his final tour and returned home, his father, mother, and younger sister.

Each man had his own way of dealing with tragic loss; some shut themselves away, some drank. His was throwing himself into his work. Zane's self-prescribed therapy was exorcising his demons by having sex with every beautiful woman who smiled in his direction.

Thus far, none of them had captured his interest enough to warrant a second thought. The possibility that he might have found one to hold his attention for more than a night or two was an encouraging one.

"Yeah. She's… different."

"Oh?" Different was good. *Maybe.* Something a tad more substantial than the vapid beach bunnies he usually went after would be welcome. A voodoo priestess or a Goth pincushion, not so much. "How so?"

Zane shrugged. "I can't explain it. She's smart and funny. Sexy as hell. No matter what I do, I can't seem to get her out of my mind."

"Sounds serious." *And socially acceptable.*

* * *

"Maybe." Zane let the word hang in the air. Was it? He'd been honest when he said he couldn't stop thinking about her. And three nights in one week with the same woman was something new for him. Usually one was enough for him to lose interest after several hours. Celeste, however, intrigued him. He wanted to know more about her; most women talked incessantly, but not Celeste. She was the first person he'd ever met that actually talked less about herself than he did. He had his reasons, of course, but what were hers?

Outside of learning the little things that drove her out of her mind with lust and made her come, he was woefully short on useful intel. He didn't even know her last name, he realized with a shock.

"Does she feel the same way about you?" Ever the lawyer, Mitch probed for information.

Zane frowned. "I don't know. She seems happy enough when we're together, but…"

"But?"

Zane rubbed the back of his neck. "But so far our time together hasn't extended past the bedroom."

Mitch's eyebrows rose. "Oh? You haven't taken her out?"

"No. I asked her to go sailing, to dinner, and a couple of other things, too, but she's always busy."

"Hmm," his uncle hummed, a telling sound that only increased Zane's growing sense of unease. "That's a switch, isn't it?"

Zane took the blow, knowing Mitch was only voicing the truth. Usually Zane was the one discouraging attempts to turn a hook-up into something more than just sex. At first, he'd thought himself lucky that he'd found someone who wasn't openly clamoring for all the extras – dinner, movies, drinks, five-date rules – wastes of time and money that would lead to good, even great sex, and then the inevitable moving on. But now *he* was the one wanting more, and if anything, his interest in Celeste had grown stronger instead of waning.

He genuinely liked Celeste – the sound of her voice, the way she smelled, her witty banter. She hadn't made any of the usual demands on him, either - beyond stretching him to his sexual limits, that was. She didn't ask a bunch of questions or try to get into his head, or whine about not going out. She seemed perfectly content to please and be pleased.

He knew exactly where to kiss her to make her melt. Just where to stroke to make her tremble with need or spill her honeyed cream for him. There was not a spot on her body he hadn't kissed, licked, sucked, and caressed.

But he had no idea what kinds of food she liked, or what type of music she listened to. Did she prefer books or movies? What did she do for fun (besides turn him inside out)? Where had she grown up? What prompted her to move? These were just a few of the questions to which he wanted answers, but Celeste had proven more than capable of distracting him whenever he started asking.

The things he did know were minimal, at best. She was obviously intelligent if she could design and build custom computer systems. Definitely not materialistic, given the lack of content in her condo. And a bit on the messy side. He had yet to see her "bed" made, and her clothes were often draped over the cardboard boxes strategically placed throughout her place. Digital equipment was everywhere in seemingly haphazard piles; though to be fair, she seemed to know exactly where everything was. Her furnishings – table, chair, and mattress excluded – consisted of moving boxes propped open and stacked on their sides like a poor man's version of IKEA chic.

Zane didn't think it was due to a lack of money, either. Anybody who could afford a condo is this community had to be pretty comfortable financially, and her clothes were well-made if not extravagant. The few items in her fridge and cupboards were top-shelf, too. Celeste had an earthy ambivalence toward material possessions, yet another thing that sparked his interest.

In short, she intrigued him enough to warrant further study. Maybe once his curiosity was satisfied, he'd be able to go more than a few minutes without thinking about her. Or wondering what she was doing at any given time. Or whether or not she might be thinking of him, too.

The irony of the situation was not lost on him.

"So what are you going to do?" Mitch's voice cut through the mental fog and returned him to the present.

As far as Zane was concerned, there was only one answer. "Keep trying."

Mitch considered him carefully for a few minutes, then nodded. "Guess I'll call Jessica and tell her you're not interested then."

Jessica was his uncle's current woman friend. From what Zane had seen of their relationship, it had the potential to be serious, if it wasn't already. "Interested in what?"

"Her daughter just moved here, and hasn't really had much of a chance to settle in or meet anyone. Jess says she's got her own business and works all the time. She hasn't even gotten around to getting furniture yet. Jess put together a small, informal dinner party tomorrow night and invited a couple of people in the hopes of getting her out and about for a few hours. She asked me to invite you, too, since you're around the same age. Thought you might be a good resource if she had any questions about local attractions and whatnot."

The wheels started turning in Zane's head, certain words appearing with bold highlights in his mind. *Just moved? Has her own business? No furniture? It couldn't be, could it?*

"What else do you know about her?"

"Relax, Zane. It's not a set-up or anything. Jess's daughter isn't really your type. She's a real sweetheart. Insanely intelligent. Quiet."

Feeling slightly insulted, Zane ignored that. He'd thought the same thing once, an eon ago. Before three nights of mind-blowing sex and this inexplicable desire for more. "You've met her?"

"Yes. She had some legal issues I helped her with."

My mother really likes him, and he's a great guy. He ... did something for me. Celeste's words echoed in his head. It was all starting to make sense. And it was far too good of an opportunity to let pass by.

"Oh. Well, count me in."

Mitch's eyes narrowed. "What about the girl you were just telling me about?"

"She's busy tomorrow night. And Jessica's your woman, yeah? I'm there for you, man."

"Thanks, Zane," Mitch said suspiciously. "It would mean a lot to Jess. Shouldn't be anything too hard. Like I said, she's on the quiet side, shy, and probably won't even stay long. An hour or two would suffice, I think."

Zane smiled in anticipation. "I think I can handle that."

Chapter 5

Zane Fagan had been a Marine for a long time. Long enough to have seen his share of life's unexpected ups and downs. So when he returned from his workout ahead of schedule to find a very attractive female backside sticking out from beneath his uncle's desk (a definite "up"), he took it in stride. Especially when he already knew that particular backside intimately.

He watched in silence as she wiggled this way and that on all fours, intent on her task. Whatever that might be. He especially liked it when she lowered her shoulders toward the ground; it made her cute little ass stick up in the air.

Zane shifted his weight slightly. It was a hell of a nice view, and brought to mind images of animalistic mounting. *Oh yeah.* It was inspiring. He knew exactly what position he would take her in next.

"Celeste?" Instinctively, Zane melted back into the shadows as Mitch emerged from the kitchen with a can of soda in hand, looking around the room for her.

"Under here Mr. Fagan," she answered in that gentle, soft voice of hers. She crawled out from beneath the desk and stood. Celeste smiled as she accepted the drink, and Zane's heart stopped for a moment; he wasn't used to seeing her in so many clothes. She wore faded Levi's, a powder blue cotton T with some kind of mathematical symbols on it, and black Chuck Taylors. Her hair was pulled back in a haphazard ponytail, if it hadn't been for her lush curves, Zane might have mistaken her for a teenager.

"Thanks," she said, taking a sip. She drank right from the can, Zane noticed. That thought came well after his brain processed her full lips touching the rim, her eyes half-shuttering, and the rhythmic movements of her throat muscles as she swallowed. *Damn, he had it bad.*

"You're good to go."

"Already?" Mitch raised a doubtful eye and looked around.

"Yep."

"But where is everything?" His eyes scanned the top of his desk. The only piece of electronic equipment seemed to be a small tablet the size of a notebook.

She grinned. "This is it. I've hidden the receivers and the routers. They're in the left side cabinet of your entertainment center." Mitch glanced over that way, his eyes widening when he spotted Zane in the shadows. Zane gave a slight shake to his head, indicating he did not want his presence known. Mitch frowned slightly.

"Is that all right?" Celeste asked, misinterpreting Mitch's expression. "I can move it somewhere else."

"No, that's perfect," Mitch responded, smoothing his features. "What's this?" He eyed the small device on his desk.

"That," she said with an excited gleam in her eye, "is the latest and greatest geek must-have. You can use it like a laptop or a tablet. Look." She picked up the device and manipulated it with a few twists and turns showcasing the full-sized keyboard in what she called "laptop mode", then flipping it back to hide the keyboard beneath the screen to use it like a tablet. "I've already loaded it up with a couple of the apps I thought you might need, based on your old machine, and copied all of your files from your hard disk and encrypted them. I installed some über-tight security, too, multi-leveled – on the drives, the files, email, and so on. Same stuff I did for NASA," she added without a trace of arrogance.

"This is wonderful, Celeste," Mitch told her.

She grinned at the praise. "Oh, and I integrated it with your home security system, so you'll always be aware and in control of what's going on even when you're not here. That is a really sweet set up you have. I've been thinking of getting one myself. Can I ask who did it for you?"

"My nephew. He's something of a security

expert. I can have him give you a call."

"That would be great, thanks."

"How much do I owe you?"

Celeste reached into her back pocket for a slip of paper clipped to a couple of receipts. "This should be tax deductible if you count it as a business expense."

Mitch looked at the handwritten summary of parts and the prices she'd paid for them. His eyes widened when he saw the total at the bottom. "This can't be right. I saw some of those things on sale for at least twice what you have here. And there's no labor cost."

Celeste looked away, embarrassed. "Yeah, well, I know where to get the components at a reasonable price. Those electronics places always have an indecent markup."

"You *built* this?"

Her face flushed and she shrugged as if it was no big deal. "Not from scratch or anything. Just started with the basics and tweaked a bit."

Mitch stared at her, dumbfounded. "Then I definitely owe you more than this. How long did you spend on it? What's the going rate for this kind of thing?"

Her flush deepened and she seemed truly embarrassed. "I'm not going to charge you for my *time*, Mr. Fagan, after all you've done for me. And...I enjoyed it, actually. It gave me something fun to do. The security system was a challenge;

your nephew knows his stuff."

"I don't know what to say, Celeste. Thank you."

"You're welcome." The grin was back. From this angle, Zane could see the prettiest pink flush gracing her cheeks.

He continued to watch from the shadows as Celeste had Mitch log on to the new machine, reset his password, and showed him how to use it with infinite patience. Brilliant lawyer his uncle might be, but he was nearly hopeless when it came to digital gadgetry. When she was satisfied he had the hang of it, she picked up her small bag and left.

Only then did Zane emerge from the shadows. Mitch frowned at the look on his nephew's face. His features, soft and kind in the woman's presence, hardened slightly as he looked pointedly at his watch. "Thought you weren't supposed to be back for another hour or two."

Zane kept his expression mildly curious, ignoring the stab of unease in his chest. "Finished early. Got a new system, huh? Looks pretty slick."

"It is. That was Jessica's daughter, by the way. I could have introduced you. Why didn't you want her to see you?"

Zane said nothing, but he didn't have to. Mitch was exceptionally skilled at reading people. "Oh, hell no, Zane. Please tell me she's not the one you were talking about last night." He winced when he saw the truth in his nephew's eyes.

"*Fuck*." He paced back and forth across the room before speaking as Zane followed him with his eyes. "Okay, look. I'll just call Jess and tell her something came up, that you can't make it tonight."

"Don't bother. I'm still going."

Mitch looked at him as if he was crazy. "I don't think that's a good idea."

"It's a perfect idea," Zane said, liking the idea more and more. He'd tried several times to get Celeste to go out with him, but she'd always had some excuse not to. A casual dinner at her mom's was the perfect opportunity to discover more about the enigmatic Celeste.

"No. End this, Zane, before someone gets hurt."

It was unlike his uncle to use such an authoritative tone with him, especially where his personal life was concerned. Mitch might give him disapproving, even pitying looks sometimes, but otherwise kept his thoughts to himself.

Zane's instincts flared to life, the same instincts that had saved his life and the life of his unit more than once, the ones he hadn't listened to on that last extraction when the orders came down. He'd known things would go bad, but his CO wouldn't listen. He wasn't in the military anymore and Zane would never ignore those instincts again.

"This is about more than the fact that she's Jessica's daughter, isn't it?"

"Let it go, Zane." Mitch focused his attention

on the tablet in his hands. "Christ, look at the resolution on this." He tapped a few things, his eyes widening at the instantaneous response.

Zane narrowed his eyes. "What are you not telling me?"

"Like I said last night, she's not your type. Let's leave it at that."

"Bullshit. You can't just throw that out there and expect me to walk away, not after what I told you."

Mitch exhaled heavily, suddenly looking weary. "*Let it go, Zane.*"

Zane faced him, his sturdy legs hip-width apart, heavily-muscled arms still pumped from his workout crossed over a substantial, broad chest.

Mitch shook his head and walked back into the kitchen. Zane followed two steps behind. Reaching into the stainless steel fridge, Mitch grabbed two beers and handed one to Zane.

"You might as well tell me now, save us both a shitload of time," Zane said, accepting the cold brew.

Sighing, Mitch took a long pull of the beer and sat down, clearly weighing his options. Zane could be as tenacious as a pit bull when he had a mind to but so could his uncle. It could become quite a battle of wills, because Zane was not backing down. The question was, would his uncle think the battle was worth it?

After all, he and Celeste were both grown,

consenting adults. It was really none of Mitch's business. He got that Celeste was Jessica's daughter, but Zane had a stake in this, too.

"Tell me, Mitch. Maybe I can help. Didn't she say something about wanting extra security? Seriously, you know I'm the best."

"This is about more than home security, Zane."

Zane pinned him with a glare that backed up his earlier words.

Mitch exhaled heavily. "Her ex is finding it hard to let go."

"She's married?"

"Was. Hence the term *ex*."

Zane pulled a chair away from the small breakfast table and turned it around, straddling it and leaning his forearms on the back. "Talk to me."

Mitch gave one last, albeit feeble warning. "This really doesn't concern you at all."

The hell it didn't. He wanted information, and his uncle had it. "Tell me anyway."

"Why?"

That was a question even Zane didn't want to answer for himself, because frankly, it scared the shit out of him. "Because I'm going to be your shadow until you do. Christ, Mitch, just tell me already."

Mitch shook his head again, then blew out a breath. "All right, but if nothing else makes it through, understand this: I won't see that girl hurt, feel me?"

Zane nodded, all amusement now gone from his face as dread began to settle in the pit of his stomach. Anything that got Mitch this upset could not be good; the man was known for his cool head and unshakable calm.

It was several minutes before he spoke. Zane waited patiently. He knew that Mitch was arranging the facts in his head, plotting out the most reasonable and concise way to present the information.

"Celeste is gifted. She has a brilliant mind, far surpassing the status quo. But socially, she lagged behind. When girls her age were dating, going to football games and proms, Celeste was attending night school. She got her bachelor's degree a couple of weeks after her high school diploma; the first of her master's six months after that."

"The first?"

Mitch nodded. "She's got master's degrees in computer engineering, mathematics, and quantum physics."

Zane whistled. The corner of Mitch's mouth twitched briefly. "Exactly. But she is quite possibly the most unaffected woman I've ever met. She really doesn't see herself as anything special."

Zane's mind was already moving ahead, trying to fill in the many blanks. "So... all work and no play?"

"Something like that. Think back to the smart girls you knew in high school."

Zane did, the images appearing as he mentally re-walked the halls. Mostly pencil thin or overweight. Glasses. Backwards, introverted, silent unless they were answering a question in class. He couldn't reconcile the Celeste he knew with any of that, except for perhaps the stereotypical disinterest in extraneous things. Celeste preferred function over fashion. She wore little to no makeup, and didn't fuss with things like clothes or jewelry, at least not that he had seen. Adorably absent minded and easily distracted. "Not seeing it."

"Exactly. Celeste's appearance has changed quite a bit in the past year or so. She's trying to re-invent herself, Zane. A fresh start, if you will."

A fresh start, Zane mused. The phrase was usually applicable when discussing ex-cons or bad relationships, and Celeste was about as far from dishonest as one could get. It wasn't much of a stretch to go from point A to point B. "Let me guess. She hooked up with the first guy who showed some serious interest."

Mitch nodded somberly. "Enter James Bradley, business man, National Guard weekend warrior. Flowers. Candlelight dinners. Chocolates. The whole nine yards. Jessica tried to get Celeste to slow down, take things easy, but Celeste had her head in the clouds. They were married within the year. A month after the wedding, Celeste moved out and filed for divorce."

"Why? The guy wasn't Prince Charming?"

Mitch snorted derisively. "Only if Prince Charming used Cinderella as a punching bag."

"*He hit her?*" Something red and ugly with sharp talons clawed inside Zane's gut. The Celeste he knew was so soft, so utterly feminine, so gentle, even in the throes of passion. How could any man even think of raising a hand to her?

"And then some. Put her in the hospital for a week. Jessica says Bradley was beside himself afterward, tried to apologize, but Celeste would have no part of it. Told him it was over, period."

Zane felt a surge of pride for Celeste. "Good for her."

"Maybe, if that's where the story ended," Mitch frowned. "Bradley contested the divorce on religious grounds. Took to stalking her, wouldn't leave her alone. When Celeste still refused to have anything to do with him, he threatened her friends, her family, her coworkers."

"Please tell me the son of a bitch is rotting in prison somewhere."

"He is, but Celeste is afraid he's going to get out somehow and come looking for her. I managed to have the divorce finalized while he's serving his term, as well as obtain a restraining order against him. She decided to move out here, to try to leave it all behind."

"*Fuck.*" Mitch's eyebrows rose. Even Zane was a little surprised at the vehemence in his own voice. "So that's what she meant when she said you did something for her."

Mitch shot him a questioning look and Zane relayed the little bit Celeste had told him when explaining why she couldn't go sailing.

"Yes," Mitch confirmed. "Jess told me about Celeste's situation, asked me for legal advice. I went one better. Glad I did, too. Bradley's a nasty piece of work, a tricky little bastard. Has some friends in high places, mostly right wing zealots, and knows how to get around the system."

Zane let the information sink in, automatically organizing it. "I can definitely help."

Mitch shifted, and by the look on his face, Zane knew what he was going to say. It amounted to a "thanks, but no thanks", which Zane found unacceptable. He might not be able to explain why he felt as strongly as he did, but it didn't have to make sense to know that it was the right thing to do.

"Mitch, I wasn't kidding when I said she's different," he said quietly. "And I *will* keep seeing her, with or without your permission, as long as she wants me. There's no place safer for her than with me."

Mitch leaned back, rolling the bottle in his hand, and considered him. Zane knew his uncle didn't know just how true his words were – there really was no place safer for Celeste than with him. Mitch didn't know the full extent of the skills Zane had acquired both in and out of the service, only that he was an expert in security and self-defense.

There wasn't a system - on the market or off of it - that he couldn't break.

"All right," Mitch said slowly. "But I meant what I said. Celeste is a sweetheart, and she doesn't need any more drama in her life. If you're unsure, best you back out gracefully now before she gets hurt."

"Fair enough," Zane said, but in his mind there was no question that he would be a part of this. The only question – the one he refused to look at too closely, was why he felt so damn strongly about it.

* * *

Celeste reluctantly pushed herself away from her keyboard. She'd stalled as long as she could, but she was out of time. Her mother meant well, but Celeste was dreading the evening. For all of her degrees and accomplishments, she had never quite mastered basic social interaction. Give her a decent processor, some components, and a few hours and she could build a system for just about anyone, but ask her to make inane, polite small talk for an hour or two and she was lost.

Perhaps she could go with Plan A: Pretend she lost track of time. It happened often enough that her mother wouldn't question it.

As if on cue, her phone rang. "Yes, Mom?"

"I just wanted to remind you about the dinner party. I know you tend to lose track of time."

So much for Plan A. "I didn't forget." *Much as I'd like to.* "I'm getting ready now."

"Excellent. See you soon."

"Can I bring anything?" Plan B involved an impromptu shopping trip to get whatever her mother might require – hopefully on the other side of town – which would reduce the amount of time she would have to spend at the party.

"Just yourself. I've got everything else covered."

And there went Plan B. Celeste ended the connection and exhaled heavily, tossing her phone on the mattress. She rummaged through her things, looking for something to wear. Jeans and one of her soft cotton tees would have been nice, but her mother was probably expecting her to show up in something more appropriate for a dinner party. Shorts were out, too, as was the one and only navy blue business suit she owned.

She finally selected a simple but classic sundress. Good enough, she thought as she slipped it on over her head. All she had to do was make it through the next few hours, then hopefully Zane would be peeling it off...

Chapter 6

It felt good to have a mission again. Downtime was nice, even necessary, but Zane could only take so much of it before he started feeling restless. A mission that utilized his skills and brought him closer to Celeste? All the better.

Zane took extra time preparing for the evening. He showered and shaved again, knowing that Celeste liked his skin smooth. He selected a pair of casual Dockers and a white polo, opting for his white leather runners. His objective was to look as low-key and boy-next-door-innocent as possible – not an easy thing for a man like Zane.

"Wow," Mitch breathed. "You look almost... non-lethal."

Zane chuckled. It was the best he could have hoped for. It was nearly impossible to completely downplay six-three, two hundred and twenty pounds of solid muscle but he had done his best. Besides, this was all for show, anyway. Celeste was already aware of what lie underneath. Literally. "Any last minute advice?"

"Celeste isn't expecting you, so you might have to do some quick thinking."

"You didn't tell her I was coming?"

Mitch shook his head. "No. Jessica told her my nephew was coming, but didn't mention your name. For all intents and purposes, I am ignorant of your... relationship."

"Does Jessica know?"

"No." Mitch ran his hand through his hair, a gesture he only made when he felt conflicted. Turning to Zane, one corner of his mouth lifted. "I do not want to be the one to tell Jessica my nephew has been sleeping with her daughter."

Grinning wryly, Zane agreed. "Probably a smart move on your part."

"Zane." Mitch grew serious again. "I like Celeste, and Jessica means a lot to me. It would devastate her if things don't work out and Celeste ends up with a broken heart. If Jessica's not happy, I'm not happy."

"I hear you, Uncle Mitch," Zane said solemnly.

"Right." Mitch eyed him once last time. "Last chance. You're sure you want to do this?"

Zane nodded. He was quite sure. *Scary* sure. He'd been on missions he'd felt less confident about.

"All right then. Let's go."

Mitch went into the kitchen briefly and returned with something in his hand. Zane narrowed his eyes. "I thought you said no flowers?"

"I said *you* shouldn't bring flowers," Mitch said, holding the bouquet of pink, white, and peach rosebuds in his hand. "You're not going as a romantic interest, remember? But it would be rude if *I* didn't."

Grumbling beneath his breath, Zane accompanied his uncle to Jessica's unit, located only a few buildings away. When Jessica opened the door, her whole face lit up at the sight of Mitch and the flowers in his hand. Mostly Mitch, and Zane realized Jessica was every bit as smitten as his uncle.

She invited them both inside. "Jessica," Mitch said, his voice smooth, "you look beautiful, as always." Her brilliant smile returned as Mitch leaned down and gave her a chaste kiss on the cheek. At least Zane now knew where Celeste had gotten her petite stature; her mother wasn't any taller than she was. She had the same hair and delicate features, too. He and his uncle apparently had similar tastes when it came to women.

"Jessica, this is my nephew, Zane. Zane, Jessica Harrison."

Zane met her gaze evenly, and flashed her his best meet-the-mom smile. "Ms. Harrison," he said politely. "Thank you for inviting me to dinner."

"It's a pleasure to finally meet you, Zane. Your uncle talks about you all the time."

"All good, I hope."

"Of course," she said with a smile, but he saw the flash of wariness in her eyes and wondered if that were completely true. Or maybe, after getting a look at him, she was questioning her decision to introduce him to her daughter.

"Please, come in."

Zane followed behind Jessica and Mitch, discreetly taking in everything around him. Within a matter of seconds, he had noted every possible entry and exit point, identified obstacles and potential weapons. It was second nature to him now. Once he was satisfied with the layout, he began to focus his attention on the other guests as Jessica introduced them.

There weren't that many of them; Jessica had kept it small, probably not wanting to overwhelm Celeste right off the bat. Jessica's neighbor Roxanne was there, along with her grown daughter Cameron and Cameron's life partner, Michelle. Jim Buchanon and his sister Kerri, both in their mid-thirties, professional investors with their virtual fingers in a lot of local pies – great contacts for Celeste. Zane's eyes narrowed when he spotted Chad Thompson, the muscled blonde pretty boy who owned the fitness place down by the beach, chatting with Celeste.

Celeste looked lovely in her light green cotton sundress and strappy sandals. Her hair was pulled back into a loose clip, various strands snaking out along the sides and framing her pretty face, making her look adorably tousled. A few thin gold bangles adorned her right wrist, but she wore little else in the way of jewelry. Her outfit was amazingly simple – and incredibly beautiful. She took his breath away.

How could he have ever underestimated her beauty? Even from across the room he could see that Celeste was tense, though she hid it well. As they made their way closer, Zane wondered what the douche bag was saying to make her so uncomfortable, and whether it would be reason enough to mess up the guy's too-pretty face.

"Chad, excuse us for a moment, will you? I'd like to introduce Celeste to someone." Jessica touched Chad lightly on the arm. Chad didn't look happy with the interruption, but Celeste's relief was obvious. Until she turned and saw Zane, that is. Her eyes widened slightly, then narrowed in suspicion.

"Celeste, darling, this is Mitch's nephew, Zane Fagan. Zane, my daughter, Celeste."

Zane kept his expression carefully devoid of recognition, but could not fully suppress the amusement in his eyes. "Celeste, I've heard so much about you."

She shifted her weight ever so slightly, as if poised for flight. "Have you?"

"Yes. My uncle can't stop raving about the system you designed for him." He thought he saw a flash of relief in her eyes.

"I'm so glad he's pleased."

"I've been thinking about upgrading myself. Perhaps you have some ideas?"

She smiled angelically. "I'm afraid I don't know anything about your needs, Mr. Fagan."

Zane pointedly ignored the warning looks his uncle was giving him. "Zane, please. And my needs are quite simple, I assure you."

Swirling amber met icy blue as their eyes locked. "Somehow I doubt that," she replied easily.

"Yes, well," said Jessica, taking Celeste's arm as she looked questioningly from one to the other, "perhaps you can discuss this later. The Petersons have just arrived and we must greet them."

"Of course," Zane said, stepping back and inclining his head slightly. Chad mimicked his actions, but looked decidedly less pleased.

"Thompson," Zane growled.

"Fagan." After flashing what could only be described as an unfriendly glance at Zane, he moved away to mingle. Zane didn't mind in the least; he didn't like Chad on the best of days, and now that the guy had been sniffing around Celeste, he was feeling downright hostile toward him.

"You're walking a thin line, Zane," Mitch warned under his breath. Zane flashed him a grin that said he already knew that the air practically sizzled when he and Celeste got within several feet of each other and he was enjoying every moment of it. So much for subtlety.

* * *

"What are you doing here?" Celeste asked quietly when she suddenly found herself alone on the balcony with Zane.

"You never told me you were Jessica's daughter," he chastised softly, ignoring her question.

Her back stiffened. "You never told me you were Mitch's nephew."

He shrugged easily, rolling those broad shoulders in one fluid movement. Celeste loved those shoulders, especially when she was grabbing on to them while he worked his special brand of magic. Heat flowed through her; it was an effort to pretend that she didn't want to jump into his arms and wrap her legs around him right then and there. The man smelled delicious; her senses already associated his scent with wild, earth-moving things.

"I would have if you would have mentioned who you were doing the system for. I'm not trying to hide anything, Celeste."

She regarded him carefully, quickly coming to the conclusion that he was telling the truth. "So… you really didn't set this up?"

Half of his mouth curved up in a heart-stopping grin. "No. I'm here because your mother invited me and this girl I've been seeing has other plans tonight."

Her lips quirked, then her expression turned dark when she looked through the French doors and spotted Chad looking for her. Zane followed her eyes. "What did he say to you before that upset you so much?"

Celeste snapped her attention back to Zane, surprised that he had noticed. "It was nothing."

Zane leaned forward so that his mouth was close to her ear. "Liar." She just barely silenced the soft whimper that nearly escaped when she felt his warm breath against her skin, reminding her of just how much pleasure he was capable of providing with that mouth. She shook herself free before the all-too familiar desire he was so skilled at calling forth gained purchase and overtook her.

"I should go mingle."

Zane grunted softly, a sound so primal and masculine that for one moment, Celeste imagined him tossing her over his shoulder and taking her back to his cave. It wasn't a wholly unpleasant thought, and sent a delicious shiver of lust down her spine.

"Okay."

Celeste turned to rejoin the party, reluctantly leaving Zane to make her mother happy and chat with the guests. It wasn't going to be easy, she realized, feeling Zane's eyes glued to her butt as she walked away.

"Stay away from him." Chad offered this little gem of unsolicited advice when he saw Celeste looking casually over her shoulder to find Zane's eyes on her. *Again.* While he'd kept a respectable distance most of the night, there were very few times when his eyes weren't on her. She did her best to pretend she hadn't noticed. Apparently Chad had noticed, though.

"Oh?" Celeste said softly, turning back to Chad and schooling her features into mild interest. "Why is that?"

Chad looked at her indulgently. He, like so many others, mistook her quiet and gentle demeanor for naïveté. It was a common misconception and one Celeste didn't attempt to disprove. She'd learned the hard way that being underestimated sometimes provided those few precious seconds that could decide the outcome of a dangerous situation.

"Let's just say he's got something of a reputation for being a real ladies' man."

Celeste smiled sweetly. "I would think people might say the same about you."

It was a deliberate stroke to his ego. Chad tried to look modest and failed miserably; Celeste fought to keep her expression neutral as Chad flexed subtly and turned slightly, no doubt gracing her with his 'good side'.

"Sometimes a man needs to do a lot of searching before he finds the right one." He looked suggestively at Celeste, as if he might be considering *her* the next possible candidate.

That was not happening. She supposed there were a lot of women who found his tanned, toned surfer look desirable, but any female appreciation she might have had for him died a quick death the moment he opened his mouth. The guy definitely didn't lack for self-confidence, and she found his rampant narcissism very unattractive. If they had been anywhere but her mother's, she would have left a long time ago. But she continued the charade, sighing softly in empathy.

"It is difficult, isn't it? So many people aren't what they seem."

"That's it exactly," Chad nodded. "Sometimes you know right off; other times, it takes a while. But don't be fooled by Zane Fagan," he added when he saw Celeste's eyes flick back in his direction. "The only thing that guy's looking for is a hook-up. Half the time he doesn't even bother buying them dinner."

So she wasn't alone, then, she thought with just a slight pang of conscience before she reminded herself that she wasn't interested in anything more, either. And she felt some inexplicable need to defend Zane. At least Zane was honest about his intentions, not like this self-absorbed poser.

"Really? He's been nothing but a gentleman to me all evening."

Chad considered this, looking doubtful at first but then nodded. "Yeah. I guess you're not really his type."

"He has a type then, does he?" she mused thoughtfully.

Laughing softly, Chad said, "Yeah. Tall, lithe blondes. Think swimsuit models." He gave Celeste a quick once over. "I think you're probably safe." He winked. "But come down to the fitness center and we'll get you looking beach-worthy in a couple of months."

Fighting a sudden feeling of complete inadequacy, Celeste reinforced her polite smile. "Well, that's a relief. Thanks for the heads-up."

She excused herself, leaving Chad behind with a slightly bemused expression, as if he was just realizing that he might have said something offensive. It took her a couple of minutes to reach her mother – she made it a point to remain as far away from Zane as possible as she did so, even though she clearly felt his gaze following her progress across the room. She had to admit, it gave her a thrill to know he was watching her, to have this naughty little secret between just the two of them.

"Thanks for dinner, Mom. This was nice."

"You're not leaving already, are you?" Jessica asked, frowning.

"Yes. "

"Please stay a little longer."

She cast a meaningful glance back toward Chad. "I can't. I've made other plans."

Jessica raised an elegant brow as her eyes followed Celeste's gaze. "What plans?"

"Nothing you need to worry about. I'm meeting a friend for coffee." She couldn't completely stop the secret smile tugging at her lips. Jessica looked like she wanted to question Celeste further, but dare not do so in the presence of the others. Looking less than pleased, she waved over at Mitch, who instantly made his way to her. "At least allow Mitch to walk you home."

"I'd be happy to do that, if it's all right with Celeste." Zane's deep voice said from behind her.

"That's very kind of you," Celeste answered, pulling her lightweight sweater over her shoulders, "but I'm meeting someone." Her eyes twinkled in challenge.

He smiled serenely in return. "Actually, that will work out well. I, too, have plans, and was just on my way out. I can walk you on my way."

"Yes, well, I suppose that would be all right, if you're sure it's not an inconvenience."

"None whatsoever."

"Who are you meeting again?" Jessica asked, interrupting the gaze they sustained between them.

"A friend." Celeste gave her a patient smile, "Don't worry, Mom. Goodnight. I'll call you tomorrow."

Chapter 7

They made it out of the building and around the corner before Zane pushed Celeste into the shadows and took her mouth in a knee-weakening kiss. "I've been wanting to do that all night," he confessed. "You look absolutely breathtaking, Celeste."

"You look pretty hot yourself," she said, nipping his bottom lip. "Even Cameron couldn't take her eyes off of you and her tastes don't run that way."

"You mean like Chad couldn't take his eyes off of you?" he growled, drawing her tightly against his aching groin.

"Just professional interest on his part," she breathed. Celeste closed her eyes and tilted her head back enough to give Zane unrestricted access to the sensitive spot beneath her ear. "He graciously offered to personally oversee a training program to have me beach-worthy in six months."

Zane growled again. "I always knew he was a fucking idiot. Come on. We'd better go or I'm going to take you right here in the bushes. Christ, you smell good."

He released her and took a deep breath in an

effort to control his baser animal urges. Taking her hand, he tugged her back onto the lighted pathway.

"My place is that way," she said, still panting lightly from that last kiss.

"I know. We're going for dessert, remember?"

"You were serious about that?" Her genuine surprise and obvious disappointment was precious. Zane laughed and pulled her along.

"You don't have to do this, you know," Celeste said quietly. They sat at a small table on the outside patio of Sweet Caroline's Pastry and Bakeshop, overlooking the bay. It was a lovely night. The skies were clear enough to see the blanket of stars above them, and a warm breeze blew off the water, bringing with it the scents of salt and sea.

Mugs of coffee and a sampler tray of signature desserts sat between them. She looked at it warily. Zane was going to give that loser Chad a good beat-down for making Celeste doubt herself. He nudged the plate of delicious pastries a bit closer to her in encouragement, taking one for himself.

"Do what?" Zane asked, popping a bite-size chunk of Baklava into this mouth.

"*This.*"

"You don't like it? We can go somewhere else."

Celeste looked down at her mug. "No, this is wonderful, but… you don't have to take me out, or waste your time and money for something I'm already willing to give you freely."

Her words cut him deeper than he wanted to admit. "Is that what you think, Celeste? That the only reason I might want to take a beautiful woman on a date is so she'll have sex with me?"

She blushed at the compliment, her shoulders lifting slightly in a gentle shrug. "Isn't that kind of the way it works?"

"Sometimes," he admitted reluctantly, though he'd never really thought about it that way. He'd always seen it as a gentlemanly thing to wine and dine a woman before seducing her. Put so bluntly, it seemed cheap and demeaning, a socially acceptable form of bartering goods for services rendered. Until Celeste, he hadn't been interested in anything more than a fleeting, physical relationship. But now...

"It's okay, Zane," she said softly.

No, it's not, Celeste," he said. "I want to do this. To just... be with you."

"Why?" she asked. Those big eyes met his, filled with curiosity and genuine bemusement.

He sat back, raised the steaming mug of coffee to his lips, attempting to organize his thoughts in a way that made sense. He opted for cautious honesty. She seemed to respond well to that. Once again, he had a feeling that his answer mattered greatly, and a lie would put a premature end to anything between them that might yet be.

"Because you intrigue me. I've never met

anyone like you. Is it so bad that I want to get to know you better?"

"I think you know me better than most," she chuckled. A pretty rose flush colored her cheeks. He loved that she was still innocent enough to blush like that, even after everything they'd done together. A small knot formed in his chest, a now-familiar warning that Celeste was different from any woman he'd ever known.

"Some parts," he agreed, matching her smirk with one of his own. "But you're kind of like a potato chip."

She raised her eyebrows, bemused. "A potato chip?"

"I can't eat just one and be satisfied, being with you is like that. What I've tasted is delicious, but you leave me craving more."

Celeste laughed at the analogy. "You're insane, did anyone ever tell you that?"

"Repeatedly," he grinned boyishly. "So?"

"So what?"

"Tell me about Celeste. Feed my Frankenstein, baby."

She laughed again, but it was softer this time. Looking down at her plate, she played with the icing on a mini-cupcake in the shape of a rose. "I'm really not all that interesting."

Zane already knew that wasn't true, but he couldn't say that without revealing that Mitch had slipped him some inside info, and he had no wish to rat out his uncle. More importantly, he wanted Celeste to trust him enough to tell him herself.

"How could you possibly know what I find interesting?"

She reluctantly conceded he had a valid point. "All right. What do you want to know?"

Sitting back, Zane sipped his coffee and pretended to think about it for several long minutes before finally asking, "What do you think of southern California?"

She blinked, surprised by his question. It hadn't been his first choice, but he'd seen the subtle shift in her body language. Her arms drew closer to her body and she leaned forward just a little, steeling herself in anticipation of something personal. Given the way she averted her eyes and licked her lips, he guessed that she was already thinking of evasive yet essential partial truths.

"Oh. Well, it's nice enough."

Zane raised a brow expectantly.

"I mean, I like the warm weather and the sunshine. Most of the people seem friendly enough, and there's great business potential for someone like me."

"But?" he prodded, sensing there was more.

"But... I like mountains. Clean air. Lots of trees and quiet and space between me and everyone else. I'm really quite anti-social. If I had better survival skills, I'd live in a cabin and do everything remotely."

She cleared her throat self-consciously, her cheeks flushing a pretty pink, embarrassed by her own TMI. "What about you? Mitch mentioned you've been staying with him while you're looking for investors for your home security systems."

"Did he now?" Zane mused, delicately avoiding her question. The truth was he found the idea of living in a secluded mountain cabin terribly appealing, even more so if it included Celeste. Saying so at this point, however, might sound suspect. And while Zane loved kissing her ass (and various other parts of her) literally, he did not want it to appear as if he was doing so figuratively. "What else did my uncle say?"

"That he's quite proud of you. He says he sees a lot of his brother in you." Zane took another drink of his coffee to help ease the sudden tightening in his throat. "He and your dad were twins, I take it?"

Zane blinked. "Did he tell you that?"

"No. Purely conjecture on my part. When he spoke of your dad, I could see a lot of emotion in his eyes, like they were especially close. And you look so much like him. It seemed like a reasonable conclusion."

"You're very astute."

She nibbled at a cream-filled chocolate square, her lashes lowering almost shyly. He felt a little twinge somewhere deep in his chest cavity. "I'll add that to sexy, smart, beautiful and incredibly sexy."

"You said sexy twice."

"So I did," he grinned unrepentantly, but was unwilling to divert the open communication they were sharing with sexual innuendo. He sensed that Celeste was not comfortable with sharing personal things, and wanted to make the most of it while he could. "So tell me, if you're not crazy about the area, why move out here?" It was a carefully veiled inquiry to see if she would willingly offer any of the information Mitch had hinted at.

She paused, choosing her words carefully. "Several reasons. My mom's here, for one. And I'd be lying if I said I wasn't curious about the man who seems to have captured her fancy these days. There hasn't been anyone she's been serious about since my Dad."

"He passed?"

"Yes."

"I'm sorry," he said, and meant it. He knew first-hand what it was like to lose a parent.

Brows drawing together, Celeste nodded, adopting Zane's trick of sipping coffee to gain a few extra moments before speaking. "I was pretty young. Seven, I think. He was killed in one of the skirmishes following Desert Storm."

"Your dad was in the service?"

"Marines."

"Yeah? Me, too."

"I know."

"How could you possibly know that?" Zane knew for certain he'd never mentioned it.

She pinned him with a patient look and her lips curved into the ghost of a smile. "Your tattoo. The one on your left bicep."

It was a classic 'duh' moment; somehow he'd forgotten the globe, eagle, and anchor tattoo, the standard Marine logo, with the words *Semper Fi* inked in script. Spending time with this woman was playing havoc with his usually keen intellect. To be fair, though, his biceps were not usually the focus of her attention when they were naked and sweaty (which, until tonight, described most of their time together thus far), and she had never brought it up. He would do well to remember that Celeste was not the bubble-headed type he was used to.

It was time to continue on. "Did my uncle pass inspection?"

"With flying colors," she chuckled. "I definitely approve. He's perfect for her."

"So you said there were several reasons," he prodded. "Why else?"

"Well, like I mentioned, it's a good place to start building some good business contacts."

"And?" he prompted.

She exhaled. "Why do I think I'm not the only one who might be considered astute around here?" she muttered. It was Zane's turn to smile serenely. "Okay," she said, taking another deep breath, as if gathering her courage.

"I'm hoping to start over. California is radically different from my Northeastern upbringing." And beachy southern California was the last place anyone who knew her would look for her.

"Why do you need to start over?"

She scratched her nail against a dark spot on the ceramic mug. "I made a lot of mistakes, some that nearly cost me my life. I'm not really comfortable talking about it, though." She glanced up at Zane to gauge his reaction. She really hadn't revealed much, but he had a feeling it was a big deal for her to even admit that much.

"I can understand that," Zane said quietly. "I've made a few mistakes myself."

She raised her eyes to his in question, but he was every bit as closemouthed about certain life-shaping events as she was. Besides, he had no wish to send her running in the other direction just yet. A woman like Celeste just might if she knew some of the horrible things he'd done in the name of freedom, acts he'd meted out in the name of justice. Someday, maybe, he might be able to share. If he ever could tell anyone, it would be someone like Celeste. Someone who understood all too well what it took sometimes to survive in an ugly world.

Her eyes were doing that swirling thing again, little ribbons of dark mahogany moving through liquid amber. He could almost see her connecting the dots as she seemed to look into his soul. Strangely enough, he allowed it, sighing. Not talking about it was one thing, but there was no way he could completely hide the damage, not from someone as intelligent and, he was realizing, perceptive, as Celeste. She hid behind that quiet gentleness, used it as a screen, but she was every bit as watchful as he was. Underestimating her would be a grave mistake.

"You're not re-enlisting." It was a softly-spoken statement, not a question. As if she *knew*. Knew the deepest, darkest secrets of his soul. And for the first time in years, something unclenched deep in his gut. She was still there, not running away, and she gave no indication of wanting to.

He shook his head, his eyes unreadable. "No. Like you, I'm starting over."

Or trying to. When he closed his eyes at night, he still heard it. The sharp staccato of rapid gunfire. The hate-filled shouts in a guttural foreign language. The screams of young women who had been abducted and brutalized, sold to the highest bidder. The knowledge that this had been what his mother and sister had faced when they had been taken by the same monsters.

He'd been overseas at the time, but he knew every last detail by heart. It had been a family vacation; his father, his mother, his sixteen year old sister. They'd woken up, eaten breakfast, then went out to do some sightseeing. His father went to take a piss, woke up much later in some rat-infested bathroom with a gash in his head. After showing photos of his missing wife and daughter, the local *policia* informed his father that they had likely been the victims of a human trafficking operation. They were sympathetic, but not optimistic.

Charlie Fagan had appealed to the U.S. Embassy, but they hadn't been very helpful, either. He took it upon himself to find them, detailing every lead in letters he sent back to Zane. Off the grid on assignment, Zane hadn't received the thick bundle until after his father's body had been discovered. His father had been shot execution style and left in his hotel room, dressed in nothing but his briefs.

The moment Zane was released from active duty, he had taken up where his father left off. Those letters had given him a good starting point, and Zane collected enough evidence to warrant official action. Because of his efforts, and because of his service record, he had been allowed to take part in the take-down.

Months later he had learned that his mother and sister were dead. Both fair of hair and skin, they had been sold to a dealer in Europe known for his sadistic tendencies.

It had broken something inside of Zane. Though the rational part of his brain knew that there was nothing he could have done, the irrational part continued to harbor guilt. If he had been there, he might have been able to prevent the abduction. If he had been smarter, faster, stronger, he might have been able to track them down before it was too late. If, if, if…

The nightmares still plagued him, the demons of the past still shredded him from the inside. He still woke up in a cold sweat, heart pounding, an inhuman roar lodged in his throat.

Except when he was with Celeste. When he was with Celeste, his demons were quiet.

They sat in silence for several minutes, each mulling over what the other did (and didn't) say.

"Do you have a bucket list?" Celeste asked suddenly.

"A bucket list?"

"Yeah, you know. A list of things you want to do before you die."

"I know what a bucket list is," he said. As often happened when he was with her, she pulled him out of his dark place and back into the present. "I don't plan on dying anytime soon."

"Me neither, but you never know, do you? I mean, it could all change very quickly, don't you think?"

Had she somehow sensed his morbid thoughts? Unless Mitch had told her what had happened – and he was certain Mitch hadn't – there was no way she could have known. Which meant her comment was based on her personal experiences, not his. It was starting to make sense. Celeste feared her abusive ex would get out and track her down.

Zane's first instinct was to ease her fears, to tell her that he would protect her, but he checked that impulse before the words made it out of his mouth.

He was reluctant to make promises he might not be able to keep. It wasn't because he doubted his ability to keep her safe; he knew beyond a doubt he could.

No, the problem was whether or not he'd still be around. According to his uncle, Celeste's ex was locked up good and tight and had a decent amount of time remaining on his sentence, a far longer amount of time than Zane had ever been in a relationship.

If he was honest with himself, he wasn't even sure he was capable of it. He only knew that Celeste had managed to hold his interest for longer than anyone else. And maybe, *maybe*, there was a chance for it to become something more. At the moment, he couldn't imagine losing interest in Celeste any time soon, but he wasn't sure enough of his relationship potential to risk getting her hopes up. This was all uncharted territory for him; he was taking it day by day. He just knew he didn't want to hurt her, and *maybe* wasn't enough to hang her hopes on.

"Yeah. I've seen it happen enough not to. Do you? Have a bucket list, I mean?"

She nodded, her eyes looking even bigger than they did a minute ago. Christ, when she looked at him like that it did something to his gut. "Want to see?"

"Hell, yeah." He couldn't have asked for a better insight into the woman currently monopolizing most of his waking thoughts. She grinned and opened her small hand purse. Her eyes glistened with excitement, like she was going to share a secret with him.

A faded photo fell out when she opened her wallet. Celeste reached for it, but Zane was quicker. An attractive woman and a young girl stood side by side on the steps of a Gothic-looking building. He recognized Jessica immediately, but not the girl next to her. Judging by the clothing and hairstyles, he would place the picture at being taken about ten years earlier. "Who's this with your mom?"

Celeste cleared her throat. "That's me," she said, her voice little more than a whisper.

Zane looked up sharply to see her face suffused with red, then looked back at the photo, his mind unable to reconcile the woman currently sitting next to him with the young girl in the picture. The girl in the photo was clearly overweight, with long, straight dark hair and thick glasses. Braces were visible in her awkward smile. Jessica was beaming, proudly holding up a diploma, the name easily identifiable: Princeton.

Celeste snatched the photo back, clearly embarrassed.

"You look different," he said simply. Celeste snorted, then immediately brought her hand up to her face, mortified. "Ya think?"

He chuckled. "You know, I was the smallest kid in my class until I hit high school. First day of my freshman year, I walked in and was promptly escorted to the principal's office. They thought I was an elementary school kid who got on the wrong bus."

Celeste raised her gaze, her eyes widening. He knew she was trying to picture him as that skinny, awkward kid he'd once been. "Really?"

"Yep. Then in one year, I shot up seven inches. It was awkward as hell; I grew so fast I actually had trouble with my balance. The next year, my testosterone kicked in and I packed on about fifty pounds and another five inches. Started growing hair in all kinds of interesting places, too," he winked.

She laughed, the last of her embarrassment fading away. There was that tug in his gut again, feeling like some kind of hero because he'd made her smile.

"So… about that bucket list. Let's see it."

Somewhat reluctantly, Celeste handed him the paper. It was well-worn, soft and tissue-like from being folded and unfolded so many times. A bulleted list in handwriting so perfectly uniform it might have been computer generated, spanned two columns. His eyes scanned the list, his amusement growing with the first few entries.

- *Get a tattoo.*
- *Get a navel piercing.*
- *Go skinny dipping.*

- *Ride a Harley.*
- *Pet a snake.*
- *Dance with reckless abandon.*
- *Go to Disneyland.*
- *Adopt a pet.*

"This is your list?" he asked. He'd been expecting her list to include items on a much grander scale, but *hell*. Most of it consisted of things regular people did every day.

She nodded, squirming a little. Zane returned his attention to the list, squinting at the singular entry crossed off.

- *Have wild hot sex with a gorgeous stranger.*

He had trouble reading beyond that line. He raised his eyes and found her looking at him intently. He held her gaze for an eternity, searching for something – anything – that might give him a clue to what she was thinking at that moment.

Is that all he was to her – an item to be checked off a to-do list? Is that why she resisted his attempts for anything more? Or was there a chance that she was willing to take things a little further?

"Are you angry with me?" she asked finally.

"No," he said, drawing the word out. "Should I

be?"

She shrugged, dropping her eyes and reclaiming her list. She refolded it carefully and put it back into her wallet. "I never expected to see you again after that first night."

Well, that made two of them. "Are you disappointed?"

She looked him right in the eye. "No. I'm not," she said firmly, clearly. "Surprised? Yes. But disappointed? No." She blew out a breath. "I think the more telling question is, are you?"

Zane might have laughed if the situation were different, the irony was just too much. Celeste was looking at him from beneath half-shuttered eyes, trying to appear only casually interested in his answer, but he knew better. Her hands clutched her little purse so tightly he could see the white skin stretched over her knuckles, and she was holding her breath as if his next words meant everything.

He was about as far from disappointed as he could get, but he couldn't tell her that. After having to deal with her ex, she'd probably be running fast and far if she had any clue just how strongly he was drawn to her. It was unnerving, even to him. So he sidestepped all that by answering, "I'm here, aren't I?"

She released the pent-up breath slowly, almost imperceptibly. The death grip on her clutch relaxed. "Yeah, you are."

Zane sipped his coffee, hiding the intense wave

of relief that flooded through him. *Crisis averted.*

Chapter 8

Mitch watched Zane in silence for the better part of an hour. His nephew was definitely up to something. There was a gleam in his eye, a sense of purpose to his movements that wasn't there a few weeks ago. While he wouldn't readily admit it, the older man had been worried when Zane first came to him a few months earlier. Despite the fact that Zane said all the right things, and did all the right things, Mitch knew he hadn't completely come to terms with everything that had happened. Sometimes Mitch would catch him staring off into space with a look so haunted it sent a shiver down his spine. It wasn't gone entirely these days, but was markedly less than it had been.

"Should I be worried?" he asked dryly from behind his newspaper as Zane gulped down a cup of coffee and shoveled large spoons of whole-grain cereal into his mouth.

Zane finished chewing, swallowed and grinned, looking every bit the devilish little boy Mitch remembered and feared had been lost forever. As concerned as he was for Celeste, he could not find it in himself to be sorry to see his nephew looking happy again. "Nope."

Mitch raised an eyebrow. "You sure?"

"Yep." Another infectious grin, and Mitch found his own lips quirking.

"Seeing Celeste today?"

"Uh-huh." His blue eyes twinkled.

Mitch lowered his newspaper and glared at his nephew, giving up all pretense of feigned indifference. "What are you up to, Zane?" he finally asked.

Zane rinsed his bowl and coffee mug in the sink then placed both in the dishwasher. His grin widened as he grabbed his motorcycle helmet and wiped an imaginary speck of dust from the surface. "I'm going to help Celeste with her bucket list."

Mitch stared at the door as it closed with a snick in Zane's wake.

* * *

Zane could barely contain himself as he made his way over to Celeste's. He couldn't remember the last time he had been so excited; it certainly hadn't been any time in recent history and definitely never over something as simple as this.

He couldn't wait to see her face. He'd texted her earlier, so she was expecting him, but he had kept the details of his plan a secret. As far as Celeste knew, they were going to spend the rest of the morning at her place, the same way they usually did. Spending hours making love to Celeste and discovering new ways to make her squeal with pleasure was definitely a great way to pass the time but today, he had something else in mind.

"Change into jeans and grab a jacket. Oh, and tie your hair back."

Celeste tilted her head inquisitively, forgetting the wireless router she'd been tweaking. "It's eighty-two degrees outside. Why would I need a jacket and jeans?"

"Because," he said with exaggerated patience, taking the device from her hand and replacing it with a helmet. She looked at the shiny black headgear, then at Zane. She took in his jeans, black leather Harley Davidson boots, black T, and the leather jacket in his hand, and licked her lips. Then her eyes widened as realization dawned.

"You have a motorcycle?"

He grinned. "I have a motorcycle."

* * *

"Quit squirming," Zane commanded much later that night, splaying his large hand across her midsection to hold her down. He used the cotton swab in his other hand to carefully clean around the fresh piercing. "You've got to keep this clean or it'll get infected."

When he was finished with that, he applied salve to the new ink on the inside of her left hip bone, his touch gentle. Unable to keep still, Celeste propped herself up on her elbows to watch and grinned at his surgeon-like precision.

It had been an incredible day. Climbing on the back of Zane's Harley, she'd snuggled up close and wrapped her arms around him, vacillating between thrilling anticipation and terror. At least until Zane stopped, looked into her eyes, and commanded her to breathe.

"I swear that you will be safe with me," he'd whispered. A sense of calm had overtaken her then; a serene peace created by the absolute conviction in his eyes. If Zane said she would be safe with him, she would be.

They'd cruised up the coastline, Celeste nearly giddy with joy. The sensation of the rumbling bike beneath her, the strength and hardness of Zane in front of her. The warmth of the sun and the rush of air as they cut through it at breath-stealing speed. The scent of salt and sea and Harley and leather and Zane…

After about an hour or so, he had veered off the highway, taking increasingly smaller roads until they came to a cozy restaurant nestled along a particularly lovely cove, where they shared a tasty lunch of fresh seafood. From there they travelled to a tattoo and piercing shop.

Zane greeted the owner as if he knew him, then explained to Celeste that they had been in the service together. Celeste half-hid behind Zane at first, somewhat frightened by Chet Graver's towering frame and shaved head. With intricate sleeves of ink and a multitude of piercings – some of which she just couldn't stop staring at – he cut an imposing figure.

She warmed up to him quickly, though. For as fierce and frightening as he was on the outside, she felt inexplicably safe in his presence. He explained the piercing and tattoo processes in detail. She had to sign a few papers, then set about choosing what she wanted. Zane watched, amused, as she took her time. It gave him and Chet a chance to catch up a little. Celeste only caught bits and pieces of their conversation, but it was enough to surmise that they had been on tour together in Afghanistan.

Zane held her hand, his eyes glittering with both approval and desire as Chet inserted the dazzling crystal navel ring. It was over so fast she barely had time to think about it before he was reclining her seat and swabbing the inside of her hip bone with antiseptic.

For this, she kept her eyes on Zane. It took longer than the piercing, but not nearly as long as she'd thought it would. Chet was very skilled, and the small heart and flower design she'd selected wasn't overly complex.

"Have I mentioned how fucking sexy this is?" Zane growled, tracing around her new adornments with the pad of his index finger, knowing full well he had. Several times, in fact.

She gave a long-suffering sigh. "Yes. But words are cheap, I thought you were a man of action."

He moved so fast she barely saw him and the next moment, she was naked and he was looming over her.

"Careful what you ask for, baby," he crooned in warning, licking the sensitive spot beneath her jaw. Spending a good part of the day snug against his hard body, watching his eyes darken with lust as she was pierced and inked... she knew exactly what she wanted. No man had ever listened like Zane had. No one had ever gone to such lengths to please her. And no other man had ever made her feel as beautiful and sexy as she felt at that very moment.

"I don't want to be careful," she hummed, threading her fingers through his dark, silky hair, every bit as aroused as he was. She tugged, not enough to hurt but enough to let him know she was needy, too. "I'm a badass biker chick now, with the ink and body studs to prove it."

He chuckled against her skin, blowing little puffs of hot, moist air. "Yes, you are. What's a boy scout to do?"

* * *

Zane flipped them over so he was on his back and she straddled him. Her amber eyes were molten, with golden flecks and red flames licking hungrily down at him. She slipped her hands under his black T and pushed upward, exposing his skin. Leaning down, she tongued one of his nipples. He groaned and lifted his head to find her watching him intently. After kissing the other side, she began to slide down his body, laving wet kisses across his heated skin while her hands blindly began to undo his jeans.

Unable to do anything more than watch – fearful that even the slightest move on his part might break the spell – his eyes bored into her. What he saw nearly did him in – amongst all that hungry desire was an uncertainty that stilled him to his core and he *knew*, just as he instinctively knew so many other things about her: she'd never gone down on a man before.

He lifted his hips, silently acknowledging her request when she began to tug the denim from his body. The feel of her soft, smooth skin over his legs made his whole body shiver in anticipation.

Celeste's hand wrapped around him and he hissed his pleasure. As if afraid to hurt him, she kept her grip loose as she stroked him, her eyes wide with discovery. Zane closed his much larger hand around hers and silently instructed her on what he liked best. Eager to please, Celeste was an excellent student.

When her lips first pressed against his manhood, Zane bucked. Her kiss was so light, but it burned him like a brand.

"Ah, baby, yes!" Her kisses became deeper, wetter, her tongue a wicked little tool surely meant to drive the last threads of sanity and rational thought from his mind.

He watched, enthralled by the sight of Celeste loving him with her mouth, the feel of her honeyed waves stroking the sensitive skin around his pelvis. "Suck me, baby, please, before I die from want of it."

She obeyed without question, drawing the thick head into her mouth. Zane cursed, fisting his hands in her hair, desperately fighting the urge to thrust right down her gifted little throat. "Fuck! So good, baby, so fucking good…."

Celeste beamed at his praise and encouragement, her eyes filled with the same desire he felt. She tried lots of different things, always watching, always gauging his reactions, and seemingly loving every second of it.

He knew he sure as hell did.

Before long, his entire body had gone completely rigid and he couldn't hold off one minute more. She squealed a little when he lifted her from between his legs and flipped her on her back. There was a brief sound of ripping foil, a few muttered oaths and then he was plunging inside her furiously.

Thank God she was so wet, he thought, nearly blind with lust and need. He pounded into her, her sheath gripping him like the most perfect, tightest fist, her feminine juices spilled out over her sex, coating the very base of his shaft and balls even as he still felt the slow burn of her saliva along the length of his cock beneath the condom.

"You are so fucking hot," he panted, incapable of mercy, penetrating her with thorough strokes and a singular purpose to brand her as she had branded him; to claim her, imprint himself on her, as she had done to him.

Her cries grew in intensity and volume as she struggled to hold on, but Zane wouldn't let her, not when he couldn't control himself. Being inside Celeste, hearing her cries of pleasure, feeling the grips of her hands made such a thing impossible. She was like the perfect storm, rolling in and over and around him, intense and all-powerful, and all he could do was ride her through it.

"Come for me, baby," he ground out, a pitiless command. "Come all over my cock!"

She obeyed without hesitation and he was following her over the edge, tumbling into the abyss. Zane thrust deep as her sheath clamped down around him like a living vise, rippling and squeezing, sucking his life and soul right out through his cock. The first jet was both agonizing and exquisite, making him shout her name even as he buried his face in her neck. He continued to thrust, each penetration drawing forth more of his essence as he held her even tighter, unable to get close enough, feeling like it would never be enough.

With one final shudder, he fell to the side, pulling Celeste with him as he fought to regain his breath.

Side by side, still joined and wrapped around each other, Zane tucked her head beneath his chin. Post-coital cuddling had never been his thing, but he couldn't imagine not doing it with Celeste. He needed the contact. Needed to feel her heartbeat pounding against his chest, her breasts pressing against him with every heaving breath.

Lying there with her, stroking her back, hearing her contented sighs, he could no longer ignore the truth. He was breaking all of the rules he'd known.

He was falling in love with Celeste.

Chapter 9

"Thank you," she whispered against his neck sometime later as she lay soft and sated in his arms.

"For what?"

"For letting me … do things."

He kissed the top of her head. "I think I should be the one thanking you, baby."

"Did I, you know, do it right?"

Her voice was quiet, her words hesitant. In the darkness, he couldn't see her, but he could sense that she was holding her breath, waiting for his answer.

"Sweetheart, if you did it any better, I'd be a stain on your carpet."

She released the breath she was holding slowly; he felt the moist heat of it against his pulse point. "I'm sure it's obvious, but … this is all new to me. I like that you're so patient with me. That you don't make me feel dirty for wanting to try things."

Zane kept the strokes along her back gentle and easy, but what he really wanted to do was crush her to him. Celeste sounded so vulnerable, it made him ache. "You're a beautiful, sexy, passionate woman, Celeste. You have nothing to be ashamed of."

She hummed and snuggled closer to him. "You

make me feel beautiful."

"You *are* beautiful."

They lay in silence for a while. "You are only the second man I've ever been with."

Zane paused as those words sank in. He knew Celeste had been somewhat innocent, but he hadn't realized just how innocent she was. "Your ex-husband was the first, I take it?"

"Yes," she admitted quietly. He could sense her putting the pieces together. "How much did Mitch tell you?"

"Not much. He said he helped you get a divorce." He might have said a little more than that but Zane had no wish to lessen her trust in Mitch, nor did he want to admit that after talking with his uncle he'd done a bit of research on his own. Spending two years searching for his own answers had given him plenty of experience; and when everything was a matter of public record, gathering pertinent intel was child's play.

"Yes," she confirmed. There was so much pain and fear in that one word, in the way her soft and pliant body tensed at the mere mention of her ex. Zane didn't want her to feel scared ever again.

"Want to talk about it?"

"Not really." Her arms gripped him tighter.

"Celeste, you're trembling. Talk to me."

She was silent so long he didn't think she would, but eventually she sighed. "I wouldn't even know where to begin."

"How about at the beginning?" he suggested, pressing a kiss to her forehead. "How did you two meet?"

In the warmth of his arms, she took a deep, steadying breath. "I was twenty-two when I met James," Celeste began somewhat unsteadily. "I was working on a joint research project at the university, and was leaving the physics building when something hit me in the side of the head. I lost my balance and fell down the steps."

"What happened?"

"The biology research facility was next to the physics lab. There were some people there protesting the university's participation in stem cell research. There were even more Bio majors shouting back. It got pretty heated, then the verbal taunts became physical. Someone threw a rock and it ending up hitting me. Anyway, the next thing I remember, James was leaning over me. He put his jacket beneath my head and wiped away the blood. He looked right into my eyes and told me how sorry he was that I had been caught in the crossfire."

"I know it sounds pathetic, but no guy had ever looked at me like that before. Like I was a woman, instead of an overweight, geeky introvert. Especially not someone like him. Tall and lean, he was handsome with dark blonde hair and brown eyes. He wasn't drop-dead gorgeous or anything, but he could definitely do a lot better than me. And I thought his eyes were so kind."

Zane started to say something but she put a finger to his lips. "Please. Let me finish." Zane kissed her finger and nodded, but made up his mind right then and there that he was going to make it a priority to show Celeste just how beautiful she was, inside and out.

"He wanted to take me to the campus clinic but the police started arriving, and I didn't want to be caught up in any of that. He offered to walk me home and I said yes."

Celeste paused to take a deep breath. Her fingers swirled in small, circular patterns over his chest. He waited, guessing what happened next.

"We started seeing each other. He was very attentive. He brought me flowers and candy and took me to nice restaurants and movies. To someone like me who'd never even had a date, it was very flattering. I was so caught up in it that I failed to see the warning signs before it was too late."

Another pause. It was an effort not to tighten his grip and pull her closer. Instead, he continued to stroke and pet, pressing a soft kiss to the top of her head. He wanted to think he was doing it all for her but the truth was, he needed the contact, too.

"James was very religious, you see. At the time, I thought that was a good thing. I mean, he had a strength of conviction I found admirable, and a clear sense of right and wrong. I didn't agree with everything he said, but I was too afraid he'd leave if

I dared to say so, so I remained quiet. He took that as agreement, I guess. But I definitely didn't share his unshakable faith in so-called 'men of God', and I guess that showed through easily enough. He took it upon himself to 'bring me into the light', as he would say."

"You don't believe in God?"

"Oh, of course I do. You can't study math and physics to any degree and *not* believe in a higher power. But I was never sold on organized religion; I considered myself more of a Deist, really. James took that as a challenge, I think."

"It was great at first. Everyone was so friendly. He took me along to church picnics and on bus trips. I felt like I was part of a big, wonderful community. For the first time in my life, I had lots of friends, people who cared about me. Or so I thought."

"Things changed the moment we got home from the wedding. Gone was the sweet man who had courted me for a year. He demanded that I quit my job and end all ties with what he deemed the 'faithless university'. I was to stay home and cook and clean and raise our children like a dutiful wife."

She sniffed, and took a breath to steady herself. "Even our wedding night was a disaster. It hurt so much. James was brutal. He yelled at me for crying, telling me that sex was only for procreation, that only whores and sinners could find pleasure in it."

"He lost his patience so easily, and nothing I

did was right. Yelling at me wasn't doing the trick, so he took his belt to me, saying that a woman's obedience in all things was holy and necessary in a good marriage. He had me believing that my unhappiness was all my fault, that I was resisting the will of God. It was a test, he said. That once I embraced my faith everything would be all right. But what he really meant was that I had to embrace his beliefs and those of his so-called church, a group of zealots who hid their fanaticism beneath layers of socially acceptable Christian values."

Her breath hitched. "It sounds so obvious now; James had fooled me right along with everyone else. I can't believe I was so pathetic…"

Zane hummed slightly in disagreement, but knew Celeste had to continue, that the worst was yet to come.

"Then one day, while James was at work, a pipe burst in the kitchen. I was too afraid to bother him at the office, and I knew he would be livid if he came home to a mess, so I called a plumber. The guy was just leaving when James came home. James saw him and misunderstood; he thought that I was having an affair."

"He beat me that night. Badly. So badly that he got scared and called the ambulance. He told them I fell down the steps. They didn't believe him, though, and when I woke up I told them what happened. All of it. The police arrested James, but his church group – those people I once thought were my friends - posted bail and he was free in just a couple of hours. I don't know what he told them, but James is a born manipulator and a consummate actor. They have no idea what he's really capable of..."

"Anyway, he begged me to forgive him, swore that it would never happen again, but I knew better. That kind, caring man I thought he was, was gone and I'd glimpsed the monster inside him. That's when things really got nasty. He wasn't content to terrorize just me. He started going after my mother, the people I used to work with, even the doctors and nurses who took care of me in the hospital. He was always smart about it, though. No one could prove anything. Some of my mother's friends helped her pack up and move and they sent me into hiding until the trial."

Celeste took a deep, fortifying breath. "I filed for divorce but James contested it, saying that no man could undo a vow made before God. He got one of the lawyers in his congregation to tie things up in a mess of red tape. I lived in constant fear; afraid to go anywhere, certain he would find me. I couldn't get a job or make friends or even use my credit cards. Eventually he went to trial for beating me and he was convicted. But I know he'll come looking for me when he gets out. And next time, he'll make sure I can't run away."

Like Hell, Zane thought. Any prior doubts he'd had about being there for Celeste flew right out the window. He still couldn't bring himself to tell her, though. Especially not when she would probably perceive it as a purely emotional response to what she had just told him.

Yeah, he was as affected as hell, but that wasn't the real reason he planned on sticking around. Part of him had realized that he was falling in love with her, and he was only now being honest enough with himself to recognize it. But again, this was not the ideal time to announce it. So instead he asked, "Isn't there a restraining order?"

"That won't stop James," she said quietly. "Nothing will."

* * *

Nearly three thousand miles away, James Bradley tried to look repentant as he silently offered thanks for bleeding hearts, overcrowded prisons and the quiet but strong presence of God-fearing Christians in key positions throughout the penal system. After serving only six months of a much longer term, he found himself before a parole board being considered for early release.

He'd been a model prisoner, after all. Both his well-paid therapist and the court-appointed psychiatrist were convinced that his horrific behavior had been a one-time aberration on an otherwise spotless record: Four-point-O student, honest business man, pillar of the community, and patriot, driven to a minor breakdown when he heard malicious rumors that the love of his life had desecrated their vows.

Of course what he had done was unforgivable, he stressed to their doubtful faces. He understood that. He agreed to abide by all terms of the restraining order, asking only that he be allowed to pay for all of Celeste's medical and legal expenses – through a third party, of course.

After a mere twenty minutes of deliberation, James Bradley was handed his personal effects and escorted to the exit where a cab awaited him.

Twenty hours and several discreet phone calls later, he was on a plane to California.

Chapter 10

Celeste flipped up the magnifying lenses of her special glasses and carefully set down the new circuit board with a sigh. Ever since her soulful confession a week ago, the bond between her and Zane had grown stronger. They still had mind-blowing, epic sex, but now he spent hours making sweet, passionate love to her, too. And no matter what they did, she couldn't manage to make herself feel bad about it. What they shared was nothing less than beautiful.

She heard the telltale ding, letting her know a new message had arrived in her inbox. It was at least the dozenth time it had done so in the last half hour, all business-related. She sighed, wishing she wasn't quite so eager, but she hadn't heard from Zane since he'd left hours earlier. Her lips – the ones on her face and the ones between her legs – tingled in remembrance of his very creative method of wishing her a good morning.

You really should play a little harder to get, she chastised herself when her heart thumped excitedly against her rib cage, spotting the email from Zane. Then again, it was email and he couldn't actually see her doing an excited little happy dance. She could read the message now, she rationalized, then not respond for a while so she didn't appear the pathetic crushing adolescent she'd somehow become.

Hey, beautiful. Check your mobile, sexy genius. I think it needs charging; my calls are going straight to vmail.

Celeste was thrilled that he'd been trying to call her and was not, in fact, growing bored with her and blowing her off as her splintered self-esteem insisted. Instantly abandoning her missive to appear less eager, she tapped out a reply, reasoning that it didn't really matter. After everything she'd told him, he was still interested when anyone else would have been running as fast as he could in the opposite direction.

Sorry. I forgot.

She could hear him chuckling in her mind, affectionately commenting about how she always seemed to forget the little everyday things. He'd reminded her to charge her phone before he left, but then he'd started nibbling beneath her jaw...

A soft ding jolted her back to the present. *They say great sex can negatively affect short-term memory.*

She grinned at the screen as she typed her reply. *You don't seem to be having an issue. Should I take offense?*

Definitely not. I was almost to my bike before I

realized I forgot to put pants on.

Celeste laughed out loud in an uncharacteristic fit of giggles. Zane had that effect on her.

As if he could see her, Zane's next message arrived quickly. *Stop laughing and start getting ready. Loose, cool clothing and comfortable shoes.*

Anticipation bubbled through her like champagne, tickling and tingling. *Where are we going?*

It's a surprise. I'll be there in an hour.

Celeste didn't bother suppressing her squeal of delight. After all, nobody was around to hear it. Zane had been full of surprises these past few weeks. He had taken her bucket list to heart. She had her tattoo and her navel piercing. Had ridden multiple times on his Harley. Gone to a zoo where they'd visited the reptile house and she'd actually *held* a python across her shoulders.

One by one he was making her dreams come true; she never knew what he was going to surprise her with next.

She pulled out her list and smoothed it on the table. Only a few things remained: skinny dipping, Disneyland, and adopting a pet.

Her whole body tingled with anticipation. She changed into shorts and a tank, pulling on super-comfy walking shoes, sighing when she realized it had taken less than five minutes. *Only fifty-five to go.*

Celeste settled down in front of the partially-built laptop again and began adding additional ports (like electrical outlets, you could never have too many USBs, she thought). When that was done, she checked her email again, even though she hadn't heard a ding.

Unable to stop herself, she re-opened Zane's most recent email chain and grinned. She'd show him. She dug the mobile out from under a series of components, verified that it was, in fact, dead, and then plugged it in. It would take a couple of hours to fully charge, but she didn't really need her phone if she was with Zane.

Another twenty minutes passed, feeling more like twenty hours. She added a few memory chips to another system. Kicked off a few custom installs of her patent-pending firewall programs. Did trivial things that didn't require much concentration, too excited to focus on anything for more than a few seconds at a time while she waited.

A mere thirty-five minutes after Zane's last email, she heard her front door opening. Excitedly, she took a minute to pull her hair into a quick clip and apply a fresh coat of gloss to her lips.

"Hello, Celeste," said an unexpected voice from behind her, freezing her instantly. "Did you miss me?"

* * *

Zane berated himself for telling Celeste to be

ready in an hour. He thought it would take him longer to finish up all the schematics for his latest system but the thought of seeing Celeste again was a powerful motivator. He briefly considered taking the bike – he loved the way she wrapped herself around him when they rode – but opted for the Shelby instead.

Ten minutes early, but unable to wait any longer, Zane rang Celeste's doorbell several times before remembering that it wasn't working properly, chuckling again about her absentmindedness about such things and making a mental note to check it out for her later. He lifted his hand and gave a series of sharp raps against the door instead.

When nearly a minute went by without her answering, he knocked again, louder this time. He leaned his ear against the door, and could just barely hear the faint sounds of music from within. He smiled when he realized it was the CD he'd burned for her, a collection of classical pieces redone by heavy metal and hard rock artists that she absolutely loved. She said the music helped her focus.

He chuckled. She was brilliant and sexy, but she was also messy and adorably clueless at times. She had probably lost track of time and was deeply immersed in some computer program. It wouldn't be the first time.

Or maybe she was taking a well-deserved nap. He had kept her up most of the night, but he couldn't summon any regret over that. It was getting harder and harder to leave her in the morning; all he wanted to do was hold her in his arms until she felt safe and wanted and yes, loved.

Reaching into his pocket, he pulled out the key she'd given him. It was a remarkable show of trust on her part, giving him access to her anytime. She'd brushed it off, saying that with his knowledge of security he could get into her place anytime he wanted anyway. It was the truth, but still, her faith in him was humbling.

Amusement quickly morphed into concern when Zane inserted the key and found it already unlocked. Why was her door unlocked? He'd stood in this very spot only a few hours earlier, waiting until he heard the locks engage before he left to go back to his place. It was something he always did, since he knew she had a tendency to forget things like that.

The hairs on the back of his neck stiffened the moment he stepped into the entryway. Something was wrong; he felt it in his bones.

Zane made a quick and thorough search of her condo. A half-full mug of coffee sat on the counter, still slightly warm. Computers in various stages of construction littered every available surface in the living areas, lights blinking and screens moving as unintelligible computer code scrolled by page after page. The soft scent of Celeste's preferred body mist – soy and honey – hung faintly in the air.

Nothing was out of place. Except Celeste. She wasn't there. Where the hell was she?

Zane pulled out his mobile and thumbed a key. The muted sound of her ringtone reached him; he found the device charging on her desk beneath a box of labeled flash drives. Picking it up, he felt no compunction whatsoever invading her privacy.

There were several missed calls, most from him. But there was one number he didn't recognize. He pressed the button that connected him directly to her voicemail, skipping over the ones from him until he got to the one he wanted.

"Mrs. Bradley, this is Carl Harmon, warden of the Stratford County Pennsylvania State Correctional Facility. It is my duty to inform you that two days ago, James Bradley was released from our facility. He failed to make the mandatory check-in with his parole officer this morning. If he violates the terms of the restraining order against him and attempts to contact you in any manner, please call this number immediately…."

Forcing himself to remain calm, Zane called Jessica, hoping beyond hope that Celeste had simply stopped over there for a quick visit. She hadn't. Then he called his uncle and the police and made a quick sweep of the grounds, only to confirm what his gut already knew: Celeste was gone.

With Mitch's connections, it only took a few phone calls to verify that less than a day after being released from prison, James Bradley paid cash for a one-way ticket from Harrisburg, Pennsylvania to LA. The warden was notified. Because Bradley violated the terms of his parole and had left the state, several other agencies were notified as well, but it was too late. Bradley's plane had landed on schedule the prior evening, where he had walked out of the airport and simply vanished.

Chapter 11

"Till death do us part," James said, emphasizing the vow with the back of his hand. The force of the blow was enough to knock her from her precarious perch on the edge of the bed and onto the floor. Her head bounced off the lamp table beside it before landing face down in the filthy avocado green carpeting.

There was nothing she could do, her limbs had long since gone numb; her wrists and ankles were securely bound with zip ties, her mouth gagged. At some point James had removed the blindfold, but it did little good. Whatever James had pressed over her mouth to render her unconscious left her feeling nauseous and fuzzy-headed. The lingering stench in the sleazy motel room wasn't helping at all, either.

Celeste tried to breathe through the stabbing along her temple, opening her eyes in an attempt to stop the horrible spinning sensation. When she spotted the healthy-sized rat peering out at her from beneath the bed, she momentarily forgot the pain and tried to rock her weight away from it. She only succeeded in making it onto her back, increasing the pulsating ache tenfold.

"When I said *my* vows, I *meant* them." Celeste heard a muffled groan like the sound of a wounded animal, then realized it was her as she choked on the blood dripping down the back of her throat. James was there a moment later, reaching beneath her shoulders to lift her off the floor. He was not an overly large man but had always been in great shape, and six months in prison had only made him stronger.

He sat down on the bed and pulled her onto his lap. He steadied her with one hand and removed the gag with the other, then pressed a cool, damp cloth against her nose. "In sickness and in health," he murmured, his actions as gentle now as they had been harsh only minutes earlier. "You look so different, Celeste. Did you think I wouldn't recognize you?"

"Restraining … order," she mumbled against the cloth, fighting the urge to retch. "Breaking… law."

"Laws!" James spat, his voice dripping with scorn. "Worthless words written by faithless men. Laws change daily, hourly, based on whims and the public opinion of the sinful. The only law that matters is God's law. You are my *wife*, Celeste. *What God has joined, let no man put asunder.*"

Celeste floated in and out of consciousness, trying hard to stay awake even as James rocked her gently back and forth. "Sweet Celeste," James whispered, his voice pained. "Why do you drive me to do such things? What part of love, honor, and obey do you not understand?"

"You … *hurt* …. me," she wheezed, the words nearly unintelligible.

"I didn't mean to," James said sadly. "When I came home early and saw that guy leaving…"

"Plumb….er".

He sighed and held her tighter. "Yes, I know that now. I was wrong, Celeste. I saw him coming out of the house… he was smiling, you were smiling. Something just snapped in me, Celeste. And then I tried to apologize, but you wouldn't let me explain…"

"Need… help…."

"I will take care of you, Celeste. We're going to start over, you'll see. I got us a special place in the mountains, just like you've always wanted. It's in Canada, so it will take a few days to get there but then it will be just you and me, Celeste, like it was meant to be. No more interference. I'll give you lots of babies, and we can be a real family, just like God intended."

Celeste tried desperately to stay awake, but it was like trying to swim against a powerful tide. Those parts of her that weren't numb hurt like hell, and unconsciousness promised a temporary respite that was getting harder and harder to resist. She wished she was stronger, or braver, but she wasn't.

James held her until the bleeding stopped,

rocking her gently and murmuring how everything was going to be all right. Celeste knew better than to disagree; it would only antagonize him, and if she sustained any more injuries there would be no hope of escape. No, the best thing she could do was remain quiet and non-combative until an opportunity presented itself. Attempting anything else at this point would be counterproductive, if not suicidal.

At least James didn't seem to know about Zane, which meant Zane was safe. She couldn't bear it if anything happened to him because of her. She'd lost track of time, but knew that several hours had to have passed. What had he thought when he'd arrived at her place and found it empty? He was probably worried, as was her mother, but at least they were safe. That was all that mattered.

With that in mind, she closed her eyes and hoped against hope that it would lull James into a false sense of security.

"Celeste, wake up, darling. It will be dark soon."

Celeste cracked open her eyes to find James pulling her still-bound wrists up over her head and securing her hands to the back of the bed frame. Then he moved toward her feet and snipped the bonds around her ankles.

"Be a good girl, now," he warned. "I'm going

to get you out of these dirty clothes and into something warmer." James quickly tugged her shorts down over her hips and along her legs. "It's going to be much colder where we're going and we don't want you getting sick."

Celeste tried in vain to move her legs, but it was no use. "Can't move..." she whispered hoarsely.

"No," he confirmed. "I gave you a mild paralytic with that last sedative; I had some things to do, and I couldn't take the chance you'd wake up too early and try to slip away on me again, Celeste. It should last another hour or so, but we'll be back on the road by then. I've already gotten us a new car and switched the plates, but we're better off traveling at night, I think. At least until we cross the border." James spoke calmly with just an edge of anticipation, as if they were going to spend the day picnicking at the park instead of fleeing the country.

"No..." Celeste knew if they made it that far, there was no hope.

"I know you still don't understand, Celeste, but you will. I thought you were the one being tested, but I know now that I am, too. The plumber, prison, finding you – don't you see? I have to prove that my love is pure."

For all intents and purposes, James Bradley looked like a perfectly normal, ordinary man. With his tan, no-wrinkle Dockers and maroon Henley, he could have blended into any crowd and not raised even the slightest sense of concern in anyone around him. But Celeste could see the madness glittering in the dark brown eyes she had once thought so kind. It hadn't been kindness at all. It had been cleverly-concealed insanity.

James exhaled, looking down at her bared legs. "You've lost a lot of weight, Celeste," he said approvingly. "You look even better than I remember."

His hand moved up at down her calf, over her thigh. "And so smooth. I know I told you to keep yourself natural, the way God made you, but I like it. See? I'm willing to compromise."

"It's been so long, Celeste. I've missed you. Once a man knows his wife, it physically hurts not to be with her, did you know that? It's God's way of reminding us of our spiritual bond through physical joining. *And the two shall become one.*"

He continued to move his hand up and down her leg, each time getting closer to the juncture of her thighs. "Mine," he said in a fierce whisper as he palmed her mound through her panties. "I was going to wait until I carried you over the threshold again, but you are so tempting, Celeste. It feels almost sinful, but you are my wife, and that makes it okay."

"No," she breathed, the true horror of his words seeping into her like ice.

James grabbed the hem of her bloodied shirt and raised it up until it bunched at her wrists above her head. His eyes glittered when he took in her lace and satin bra. "So pretty..." he said, tracing the outline with his fingers. "You will not deny me this, Celeste. It is a sin for a woman to deny her husband his marital rights."

Placing his fingers at the center of her bra, he flicked once and released the clasp, then peeled back the sides from her breasts with nothing less than reverence. "So pretty," he repeated, cupping first one, then the other, pleased when she still overflowed his palms. "I can't wait to watch our children suckle at your breasts, Celeste."

He took another wet cloth and began to wipe the dried blood from her skin carefully, thoroughly cleaning her breasts before working downward to her belly. His hand froze right over her navel and he let out an evil sounding hiss as he noticed the piercing there.

The roar that came after was enough to rattle the lamps on the night tables. *What have you done?*

Her panties were suddenly torn from her body and she felt his fingers over her tattoo. His voice was little more than a choked gasp as he roughly flipped her over, wrenching her shoulders in the process as he examined her back for more markings.

"You have defiled yourself!" he said, the familiar maniacal gleam re-entering his eyes. "How could you let a man do this to you?!"

The sound of the bedside light crashing to the floor had Celeste trying to burrow into the bed in an attempt to protect herself, but she was barely able to move more than her head. She braced herself for the blows she knew would be coming any minute.

It took several moments for her to realize that someone was pounding at the door. Celeste lifted her head from the pillows and screamed as loud as she could, hoping that whoever was at the door would realize something was wrong and call the police. The sound brought James' attention back to her and he slammed his fist down hard on the side of her face. The crack was audible and Celeste's head snapped with the impact. She fell face-first into the pillow, and didn't move or cry out again.

* * *

Zane forced himself to take a deep breath, swallowing the panic that threatened to overwhelm him and calling upon his inner discipline as he crept around the corner toward his target. This wasn't a training exercise, and the people involved weren't nameless, faceless strangers.

The exact situation within was unclear; the door was closed, the drapes were drawn. From the room to the left, a television game show host droned on; from the one on the right, a particularly spirited tryst was clearly audible through the low-quality door. The only functional illumination on this side of the building – a single exterior light on the corner - flickered in the darkness, off, then on, then off again.

What he wouldn't have given for a thermal image scanner or some high-tech receivers at that moment! Zane paused, his body hugging the shadows, and focused. The murmur of voices - one male, one female – was barely audible. The female's he recognized as Celeste. She was both alive and conscious, and that filled him with both relief and a renewed sense of hope.

That relief was short-lived when the man's voice suddenly exploded in rage, followed almost immediately by a loud crash. Celeste's terrified scream rent the air, and Zane no longer cared about anything except getting to her. Sig in hand, finger on the trigger, his turned his body and delivered one powerful kick to the flimsy door.

The door flew open, the wooden frame around the outside splintering under the force of the kick. Zane rushed into the room and came face to face with a stunned James Bradley. Bradley reached back, presumably for a weapon. His peripheral vision affirmed that Celeste was not in the direct line of fire, Zane didn't hesitate. He squeezed the trigger twice in quick succession, firing once in the head, once in the heart; both lethally accurate kill shots by an expert marksman.

James Bradley slumped to the floor, landing with a sickening thud. After confirming that he was no longer a threat, Zane stepped over his body to get to where Celeste lay motionless on the bed.

"Celeste. Celeste, baby. It's over. It's going to be okay."

Tucking the gun into the back of his pants, he pulled out his Ka-Bar and sliced through the ties around her wrists. Tinged a sickly purplish-blue, her hands dropped limply to the bed. She didn't answer; she didn't move. She didn't acknowledge his presence at all.

Panic shot through him; his heart rose up into his throat as he took in her bruised, battered face and the blood. *No!* Zane refused to accept what his brain was telling him. *He couldn't be too late. Not again.*

His first impulse was to turn her over, but his field training kicked in, his instincts warning him not to move her until he assessed the situation. With trembling fingers, he touched the pads of his index and middle fingers to her neck. He held his breath until he found a pulse. Celeste was alive!

Exhaling in relief, Zane did a quick but methodical exam, his inner rage growing with each new bruise and scrape he uncovered. Celeste remained unconscious, and was unable to provide any information on the extent of her injuries, but given the swelling and bruising between her jawline and collar bone, a broken or fractured neck was a very real possibility.

He pulled the covers up over her naked body as

far as he could, wishing he could do more as he dialed 911. He dared not move her just yet; even the slightest shift could result in irreversible paralysis. Very carefully, he ensured that she had enough room to draw breath, then dropped beside the bed, praying for the paramedics to come in with the backboard as quickly as possible.

Chapter 12

If she never woke up in a hospital again, it would be too soon, Celeste thought once she was aware enough to recognize the beeps and whirs and sterile white walls.

"You're finally awake, I see," said an unfamiliar voice, and then there was a shadow over her face and a bright light shining in her eye. She tried to turn away and couldn't, so she squeezed her eyes shut instead.

"Please open your eyes, Ms. Harrison. I need to check your pupils."

"Hurts," she croaked. It came out sounding like "urs"; her jaw didn't want to cooperate. The doctor, however, seemed to understand.

"I know, and I'm sorry about that. Tell you what. We'll turn down some of the lights and allow you to get used to that for a few minutes, then try again, all right?"

"Mm'kay."

"We had to set your jaw, so talking will be difficult for a while. Unfortunately, it looks as if you might have sustained some nerve damage along your wrists as well, but early indications are that it is only temporary. I'll have the nurse bring you a pad and pencil later, but for right now keep your answers to one word and don't strain yourself." From the sound of his voice he had moved away and come back again. Through her closed lids she could tell that the room had dimmed. She attempted to open her eyes again, slowly. A blurry form appeared, looking older than his voice suggested, with neatly trimmed salt and pepper hair and silver-rimmed glasses circling eyes the color of faded denim.

He gave her an encouraging smile. "Do you know where you are?"

"Hosss-i-tol."

"Yes, good. You're in Shelbyville Medical Center, and my name is Dr. Giamatti. What is your name?"

"Celeste."

"Excellent. You've been in a medically induced coma for three days, Celeste, so that we could reduce the swelling in and around your upper vertebrae and evaluate the damage. It's also why we have you restrained, so you don't inadvertently exacerbate your injuries. Do you understand?"

"Mm'kay."

"Good girl. I'm going to try to look into your eyes again now. I'll make it as quick and painless as I can." He leaned over the bed, and shone the penlight in her eyes again. It still hurt, but not as much as it did the first time.

"Very good," he murmured, moving to the other eye. "Hang in there, almost done. Do you remember what happened?"

"Szames."

"James Bradley is the one who hurt you?"

"Yes."

"The police have a lot of questions for you, Celeste, but I'll keep them at bay for as long as I can to give you a chance to get your bearings. In the meantime, there's a young man here who is very anxious to see you. He hasn't left your side since he brought you in."

"Hey, beautiful," said a deep, gravelly voice. In her peripheral vision, she saw slow, easy movement from her right, getting closer then Zane's face appeared. He looked so tired, as if he hadn't slept in days. Dark smudges encircled his clear blue eyes, and chestnut-colored stubble adorned his jawline and cheeks. He was such a welcome sight that a wave of emotion rose up inside of her.

"Hey, hey," he soothed, his expression worried as he gently wiped the tears from her eyes. "Don't cry, baby. It's okay. Everything's going to be okay now…"

Zane remained with her while the police asked their questions. He held her hand, alternately stroking the back with his thumb or squeezing lightly in encouragement. She drew strength from the warm solidity of it, from his very presence. Slowly, and with some difficulty, she managed to convey what had happened. Zane filled in a lot of the gaps with accurate guesses, so all she had to do was answer yes or no most of the time.

The worst part was when she had to describe the events that transpired in the room. There were a lot of embarrassing questions, and answers she wished she didn't have to provide, but she understood that it was necessary. Zane's blue eyes turned hard, his expression like stone at some parts, but throughout it all, he kept his touch gentle, making little circles on her hand. It seemed to calm and center them both.

After what seemed like forever, the policemen thanked her and left. She was exhausted, mentally and physically. Zane dipped a clean cloth in a glass and dribbled cool, clear water over her lips and into her mouth. It was done with such tenderness that she almost started crying again.

"Tell me," she said. While the police were there they had only talked of the abduction and the time up until Zane arrived. No one had mentioned what happened after she lost consciousness, but she could guess.

Zane took a few breaths before answering. "Bradley's dead."

Celeste closed her eyes, feeling an overwhelming sense of relief. "You?"

* * *

Zane didn't answer right away, not knowing how she would respond. Dread pooled in his stomach. Celeste was such a gentle soul. How would she feel about the fact that he had shot a man in cold fury, two shots meant to kill instantly? Or the fact that in his mind's eye, he envisioned shooting the rotten bastard over and over again, taking savage pleasure in watching him go down, cursing him to the worst pits of hell?

He started to pull his hand away, but she gripped it. It wasn't enough to hold onto a paper bag, but he felt it just the same.

"Yes. I killed him."

Celeste looked into his eyes, saw everything he couldn't say. "Thank you."

Zane blinked, certain he had misunderstood. "Saved me," she said quietly as the sedatives began to pull her under. It was her last three words, spoken just before her eyes closed that struck him the hardest, though.

"I... love... you."

Zane closed his eyes as exultation rushed through him. She'd had a glimpse of the cold, trained killer inside of him and didn't hate him for it. Dare he hope that he had found someone who could love and accept all of him, the good and the bad? The dark and the light? A woman who wanted him for more than just the good times and pleasure he could give her?

But even as his spirit soared with that possibility, the reality of the situation shackled itself to those hopes and pulled them back down to earth. Celeste had just been through a very traumatic incident, and she was pumped up with powerful pain killers. She wasn't exactly thinking clearly.

Oh, he had no doubt that in that moment, she had spoken the truth. Lying was just not in Celeste's nature. But he also knew that words spoken under the influence of happy drugs or in the heat of passion were not entirely reliable, no matter how much he wanted to believe them. When the smoke cleared and all was said and done, when her emotional state leveled out, the depth of those feelings might fade as well.

Did she care for him? Yes, absolutely. It was in her smile, her laugh, her touch, the way she looked at him. But did she feel the same inexplicable connection that he did? The one that said she was the other half of his soul? Maybe. Or maybe those stars in her eyes weren't based in reality, but on an illusion. There was no doubt she had a skewed perception, seeing him not as the man who had failed to protect her, but as some kind of heroic white knight riding in to rescue her from the evil villain at the last minute. She certainly wouldn't be the first woman to fall in love with a romanticized ideal. And he was no damn hero.

The raw truth was, if he held her to those

words, spoken under obvious duress, he was no better than Bradley.

Zane's heart ached, but he knew what he had to do.

Chapter 13

"Where are we going?" Celeste asked when Zane drove past the exit to her place.

He glanced over, giving her the first genuine smile she'd seen on his face in over a week. "It's a surprise."

"What kind of surprise?"

"If I told you, it wouldn't be a surprise now, would it?"

His smile faded as quickly as it had come. His gaze swung back to the road; his features returned to the neutral mask he'd been wearing more often than not. She understood; he didn't like looking at her in her current state. When he did, his eyes lingered on the bruises, the bandages, the cervical collar and brace she would be required to wear for several weeks.

She didn't care for it much either, but she chose to focus on the positive. She was alive, expected to make a full recovery, and James Bradley would never hurt her again – thanks to the wonderful man currently sitting beside her.

She reached over and covered his hand currently palming the head of the stick shift. Most, but not all of the feeling had returned to her hands, the damage a direct result of the ties James had used. The doctor said she would regain full dexterity, for which she was grateful.

For a moment, he tensed, then enveloped her hand in his. It was a loose hold, so much gentler than what she was used to with him.

"It's okay, Zane," she said, giving his hand a squeeze. "I'm okay. Because of you."

He gifted her with another smile, but this one was tight and forced. When he pulled his hand away to make the turn, Celeste didn't try to reclaim it. She folded both hands in her lap and turned her gaze out the window.

Zane was pulling away, distancing himself; she could feel it. Celeste blinked away the tears suddenly pooling in her eyes. Maybe he just needed some time to process everything. Maybe the situation had brought back unpleasant memories.

Or maybe, said a little voice in the back of her head, *he's just done.*

She didn't want to believe that, but it was a distinct possibility. Ever since she'd said those fateful words to him, told him that she loved him, things had been different between them. It was the truth, though. Somewhere along the line, her bucket list walk on the wild side had become something so much more.

Zane hadn't spoken the words back to her, but she hadn't expected him to. She believed he loved her, and that he might not have realized it yet. That was okay. As long as he did eventually, she could be patient.

Before too long, Zane slowed the car and turned into a lot next to a big white building. Celeste read the large letters painted on the side. "Fulton County Animal Shelter? What are we doing here?"

"Bucket list, remember?"

That's what this was about? Celeste mentally recalled the remaining items on her list. Given her current state, Disneyland and skinny-dipping were out of the question. That left…

* * *

"Adopt a pet?" She couldn't turn her neck to look at him, so it was her whole body that twisted in his direction. Her eyes were so big, so bright, if felt like a knife to his insides.

"Yeah, why not?" he slid smoothly out of the driver's seat and went around to the passenger side to open the door for her. He offered his hand to help her out but dropped it the moment she was on her feet. He didn't miss the hurt in her eyes or the slight frown as he did, though. She didn't understand, which made it so much harder.

With a hand resting gently on her lower back, he guided her inside. The place was airy and clean, the light smell of lemony-scented disinfectant tickling their noses. One wall was filled with photos of happy smiling faces clutching new furry (or sometimes scaled) family members.

"Can I help you?"

"Yes. We – I mean, she – is interested in adopting a pet."

The receptionist, a middle-aged African American woman with a kind face, smiled warmly. She didn't even flinch at Celeste's outward appearance, which immediately earned Zane's respect. He'd wanted to beat down everyone who had gawked, stared, or openly gaped at Celeste since she'd been released from the hospital, but had made do with glaring at them until they turned away. The attention made Celeste uncomfortable, and anything that made Celeste uncomfortable was unacceptable.

That included his own recent behavior, of course, but he was going to rectify that very soon.

"Well honey, you've come to the right place. What are you looking for? Cat? Dog? Bunny? Snake?"

"Oh, no snakes," Celeste said quickly. "Definitely something furry."

"High on the snuggability scale, got it," the woman grinned. "My name is Lillian, by the way."

"I'm Celeste, and this is Zane."

"Come on back, then, and let's see what we can do."

The moment the woman opened the door, they

were hit with a wave of excited barks, yips, and meows. They paused only a few feet in, taking in the huge room filled with dozens of cages. Some big, some small, but nearly all were occupied.

"There are so many," Celeste breathed.

"Yeah," agreed Lillian, a note of sadness in her voice.

"Where did they all come from?"

"Some were abandoned, some probably runaways. People move and can't take their pets with them, or have kids with allergies. There are as many reasons as there are stars in the sky, honey, but it all boils down to what you see here."

Zane saw the look on Celeste's face, and knew she was overwhelmed. "What do you think, Celeste? See anything you like?"

"All of them," she whispered. "How can anyone choose just one?"

"Most people who don't have something specific in mind walk around, look for a connection. It's a lot like true love," Lillian said, glancing between the two of them. "When you find the right one, you'll know."

The color rose in Celeste's cheeks, but she said nothing. She didn't have to; her eyes said everything for her.

"Sounds like a plan," he said. Again he saw the brief flash of hurt, but to her credit, she smiled at Lillian and said, "Okay, let's do that."

They walked around the room once, then again.

Celeste paused a few times to take a closer look, but on the third pass, she stopped in front of only one cage. A rather large Shepherd mix sat in the far back corner, staring back at her with soulful brown eyes.

"What's his name?" Celeste asked.

"Jax."

"Hi Jax," Celeste said softly.

The dog leaned forward and sniffed, then gently licked Celeste's fingers. "What happened to him?"

Lillian's face clouded over. "Jax belonged to an elderly woman; her kids put her in a nursing home and dropped him off here. He's a good boy but very shy. Most people walk right past him."

"Can you let him out for a minute?"

"Sure, but don't expect much," Lillian said, reaching over to unfasten the catch. "He's not very social."

"That makes two of us," Celeste said softly. With careful movements, she went down onto her knees. After a few seconds, Jax stood and slowly made his way out of the cage. Zane and Lillian watched as the dog sat down in front of Celeste. She stroked his fur and scratched behind his ears; Jax reward her by nuzzling her and giving her a lick on the cheek.

"Looks like we've found a winner," Zane said. He liked the dog. As gentle as he was with Celeste, he looked intimidating, and Shepherds had a reputation for being fiercely protective of those they cared for. Celeste had already won him over.

"He's beautiful. But I'm not sure I can take care of him," Celeste said with regret. "I'm not in the best shape right now."

"Oh, Jax doesn't need much. He's very smart and fully trained. If you can manage a walk once or twice a day, you'll do just fine."

"I think I can manage that," Celeste said. "What do you say, Jax? Want to blow this popsicle stand and come home with me?"

Damn if the dog didn't give her a big canine grin and cover her face with kisses, making Celeste laugh. "I guess that settles it, then."

"Excellent. Follow me, and we'll do the paperwork."

Two hours later, Zane pulled up in front of Celeste's condo. Jax leaped out of the back seat, proudly sporting his new collar and tags, following Celeste right in like he owned the place. It hadn't taken long for the dog to become her shadow. If she was out of his sight for even a minute he went looking for her. Zane knew exactly how he felt.

After the animal shelter, Zane had driven them to one of the big-chain pet stores, and the three of them had combed the aisles. The smile on Celeste's face was worth every second. It took four trips to empty his trunk of all the new supplies they'd purchased: dog food, chew toys, stainless steel bowls, brushes.

"Will you stay for dinner?" Celeste asked when they'd brought everything inside. Jax, having sniffed the entire place, had settled contentedly on his new deluxe, super-sized doggie pillow with his new bone.

"I thought your mom was coming over."

"She is."

"You two should have some mother-daughter time. I know she's been worried sick about you."

Celeste murmured in agreement, but he could tell she was disappointed. "Maybe you could stop by later?"

Damn it. "I don't think that's a good idea, Celeste. You need your rest."

"All I've been doing is resting, Zane," she said, her mouth settling into a pout that made him want to kiss her senseless. Then the corners quirked. "I promise I won't try to jump you."

He choked, his throat making a slight strangled noise. Celeste reached over and patted his back while Jax paused mid-chew and regarded him with curious eyes.

"I'm kidding, Zane," she said. "But we could snuggle and maybe watch a movie or something."

"On what? You don't have a couch or a TV."

Celeste's smile faltered. "No, but I do have a comfortable mattress and a laptop capable of streaming."

"Not tonight, okay? I've got a lot of work to do. I fell way behind the last week, spending so much time at the hospital…"

"Oh. Right," she said softly. Her eyes lowered and she stepped back, making him feel like the biggest ass on the planet.

"Celeste, I didn't mean it like that."

"I know. I understand. I've probably got a mountain-sized backup myself."

They stood there like that for a few minutes in awkward silence, a first for them. Leaving her was the very last thing he wanted to do, but the one thing he knew he had to do. Thankfully, the doorbell rang. In a flash, Jax was up, standing protectively in front of Celeste and looking toward the door.

Celeste gave him a reassuring pat on the head. "Come on, Jax. Time to meet my mother."

Zane used that as his cue to exit. After greeting Jessica, he turned to find Celeste looking at him with those big eyes, filled with questions he didn't want to answer. He leaned down and placed a chaste kiss on the top of her head. "Goodbye, Celeste."

She blinked; his choice of words was not lost on her. She swallowed, hard, and blinked again. He waited for her to say the word back to him, but she didn't.

Zane walked to his car, feeling her gaze burning a hole in his back. He didn't turn around, but he did glance in the rearview mirror as he drove away to see her front door slowly closing.

Chapter 14

Two Months Later

"How is she?" Zane jumped to his feet and asked the question before his uncle had even fully closed the door.

Mitch tossed his keys on the table and walked right past him. His face was as expressionless as stone, giving nothing away. "You're back. Did you find the answers you were looking for?"

"It was business. You know that."

"What I know is that right after Celeste came home from the hospital you blew town on some bullshit excuse."

"It wasn't bullshit. Damn it, Mitch, you know I need some serious investors if I'm going to get my own business off the ground."

"You've got a hell of a sense of timing, Zane."

No, Zane thought, it had been the perfect time to walk away. Before he did something *really* stupid. Unfortunately, his head hadn't been in the right place and he'd blown the first two loan interviews. The rest of the time, he'd been crashing at Chet's; at least he had a new tattoo to show for it.

"You didn't answer my question. How is Celeste?"

"Why don't you go see for yourself?"

Zane scowled. "You know I can't do that."

"No, I don't know that. You're the only one who seems to see any reason behind your completely illogical behavior."

Illogical? Zane fought the sudden urge to laugh. As if anything logical had happened since Celeste's appearance. He'd met the only woman he'd ever considered spending the rest of his life with. Fell madly and insanely in love with her and did everything he possibly could to make her do the same. Then killed her psycho ex and held her hand through a broken neck and jaw while having to hear in gory detail just how crazy the sick fuck was. Where was the logic in any of that?

At least Zane had a reason for walking away, refusing to see Celeste. Hands clenched into tight fists at his side, he spat out. "Celeste understands."

"The hell she does!" Mitch's voice raised. As if he'd been viewing Zane's thoughts, he said, "You do everything you can to get into her bed and her heart, save her from the bad guy, and then, after she's lying in a hospital bed and tells you that she loves you, you just walk away?!? *Who could possibly find any sense in that?*"

Zane sank down in the chair and placed his head in his hands. In his mind it made sense, but when Mitch put it out there like that, he felt like such a rat bastard. "What does Celeste say?"

"She says... ah, fuck it. You want to know what she says, go ask her yourself."

* * *

Mitch went into his bedroom and closed the door, angry and frustrated because Celeste wasn't saying *anything*. But the sadness in her eyes spoke volumes. Both he and Jessica had tried to talk to her, but she was being stubbornly close-mouthed, refusing to discuss exactly what had transpired between her and Zane, insisting that she was fine when it was so obvious she was anything but.

Twenty minutes later he emerged, feeling somewhat calmer. His hair was still wet from his shower, and he'd changed from his three-piece court-appearance suit into casual jeans and a USMC T-shirt.

Mitch took one look at Zane, still in the same position he had left him in, hunched over in the chair with his head in his hands. Anguish and pain rolled off of him in waves; he was obviously suffering every bit as much as Celeste. She'd retreated far into herself, physically there but mentally and emotionally closed off to anyone but her dog. She was going through the motions for her mother's sake, but even that wouldn't last much longer. If Zane didn't do something soon, Celeste would be gone. Nobody wanted that to happen.

"Zane. Talk to me. You do love her, don't you?"

Zane lifted his gaze to his uncle's. Mitch was stricken by the sheer misery he saw in the younger man's face. "More than my fucking life."

"Then what's the problem?"

Zane exhaled heavily. "I love her *too* much. Can't you see? Celeste already had one psycho in her life. She doesn't need another."

Mitch couldn't have been more stunned if Zane had hit him upside the head with a two-by-four. He sank down onto the sofa across from Zane. "What?"

Torment roiled in his nephew's eyes. "Do you know how I was able to find her?"

"You called in some favors, got a lucky lead from the rental place. Used the built in GPS to track the car to the motel."

It was the story Zane had told the police. Mitch had been present for most of the questioning, acting as unofficial counsel. Zane hadn't been charged with anything – it was clearly a case of self-defense, especially with the unregistered gun they found in James' hand – but there was still a lot of paperwork involved.

Zane shook his head, looking as miserable as Mitch had ever seen him. "No. I called in all those favors after I already knew where she was."

"Then how did you –?"

"I tracked Celeste, not the car." Zane stood up and paced around the room while Mitch watched him warily. "When I took her for her tattoo, I had my buddy Chet chip her."

"You *what*?"

"Fucking psycho, right? After you told me about her ex, I did a little research."

* * *

What Zane had found made his blood run cold, and he'd formed the same opinion Celeste did long before she poured her heart out to him – when Bradley got out, he would come after her, and no piece of paper on file in a courthouse somewhere would stop him.

Mitch knew that, too. Zane could see it in his eyes. "I couldn't take the chance that Bradley would take her somewhere where I couldn't find her again." At that point, the intensity of his need to protect her had surpassed his uncertainty over their future. Even if things didn't work out between them and he wasn't around, he wanted to be able to find her if he had to. He had already lost people he had cared about because he hadn't been able to find them in time. He wouldn't live through it if it happened again.

His uncle looked contemplative; Zane knew he was rearranging all the pieces, connecting all the dots. "Does she know?"

"I didn't tell her at first, afraid of what she'd think. Afraid that she would see me as another psycho she needed to run from." He paused, pacing back and forth several more times under Mitch's close scrutiny. "But then, after she said those words to me in the hospital, I had to tell her. Blurted it all out. I thought she'd hate me…"

"But she didn't, did she?" Mitch guessed.

"No. Jesus Christ, Mitch, she looked at me with so much fucking love in her eyes I thought my heart was going to rip right out of my chest and fall into her hands. She says if it wasn't for that chip, she would have been dead by then. Or wishing she was."

"So where's the problem?"

"Don't you see? I would do anything to keep Celeste safe. *Anything*. Including doing shit like having her microchipped without her knowledge so I would always be able to find her." He cast tormented eyes at Mitch. "I'm no different than the sorry fuck who terrorized her because he was obsessed with her."

Mitch pinned him with a glare that lasted several minutes. Zane had turned away after the first minute or so, but still felt the intensity boring into the top of his hung head.

"You're an idiot."

Zane whipped his head up, finding his uncle looking both angry and disappointed. "You did those things because you care more for her safety and protection than you do for yourself."

"Bradley loved her, too," Zane argued.

"Enough that he would risk everything to be with her."

"Zane, listen to yourself! Bradley was mentally unbalanced. With Bradley it was all about control, all about what *he* wanted. He said he loved her but do you think any man that really loved her could bash her face in like that, break her jaw and neck?"

Zane winced, but Mitch kept going. "You were only interested in being able to protect her. Goddamn it, Zane. The fact that you are willing to sacrifice your own happiness for her just proves how different you are from Bradley. Do you think he would just walk away, leave her be, because he thought that's what was best for her? He didn't, did he? No. He followed her across the country, kidnapped her against her will, drugged her, and beat the living shit out of her. Thank God you do love her, or I'd be standing with Jessica crying over Celeste's grave right now."

Mitch was on his feet now, too, getting right into Zane's personal space. "Understand this, if nothing else: for the past eight weeks she's been trying to recover again, but she can't. Because she needs you and she doesn't have you."

Zane bristled. "I will always be there for her if she needs me."

"Bullshit. Maybe you aren't so different from Bradley after all, except the pain he inflicted was swift and brutal. You're killing her slowly, from the inside out."

"I love her!" Zane shouted. "Goddamn it, can't you understand that I'm doing this for her?!"

"Doing what?! Abandoning her when she needs you? *She loves you.*"

"Of course she *thinks* she loves me," Zane spat out. "I was her white knight in shining armor."

Mitch took a step back and blinked. "You honestly believe that?"

The rage drained away. "I believe she is confused. She was lonely, I came along and showed her a good time. Did stupid little things that meant the world to her, made her feel special when no one else did. Then I'm the one who killed the bad guy and saved her. What do you expect her to feel?"

Realization dawned in his uncle's eyes. Finally, he was beginning to understand what had motivated Zane to do what he did. "You're afraid."

"Hell yes, I'm afraid. Scared that one day she's going to wake up and realize that she's too good, too smart for someone like me. That with her gentle soul and big heart she deserves a better man. That everything she is feeling now is only temporary, a natural reaction to someone who blindsided her with romance and chivalry and all that romance novel crap."

He paused to suck in more air, since his chest felt like it was caving in under the weight of the pain that admission had cost him.

"I want her, Mitch. I want her so bad I can fucking taste it. But even more than that, I want it to be real. And I want her to be sure."

"So … you're staying away to give her time to think," Mitch said slowly.

Zane nodded. "I explained all that to her." He looked at his uncle. "I told her to give it six months. If, after that time, she's still interested, to call me."

"Six months is a long time."

"No," Zane said miserably. "Six months is fucking *forever*."

Chapter 15

By mutual agreement, Zane stopped asking Mitch for updates on how Celeste was doing. For a few weeks, Mitch would occasionally mention something noteworthy. Zane knew, for example, that Celeste and Jax were inseparable and took daily walks in the park. He also knew when the doctor told her she was no longer required to wear the special brace around her neck. But before long, Mitch wasn't mentioning much of anything.

Zane would watch her sometimes, when the need grew too strong and he needed a fix. Sometimes he'd sit for hours in the shadows of the trees hoping to see her appear for a moment or two on her balcony. Other times he'd don a baseball cap and lurk in the bushes around the park to watch when she and Jax came out to toss a ball or Frisbee. Occasionally, he'd drive by her place during route times and catch a glimpse of her greeting the UPS and FedEx trucks; Celeste received deliveries and sent packages out almost every day.

It was Zane's way of centering himself, of assuring himself that there was still hope. If Celeste could find the strength to recover and go on, then it was worth it – every day, every hour, every minute of personal sacrifice.

It was, quite possibly though, the hardest thing he had ever done. Each time he saw her, it took his breath away. Every time he heard her voice, he'd close his eyes and let it wash over him. And, on those rare occasions when he caught the faint scent of her on the breeze, he'd inhale deeply and imagine she was next to him again. He hated the haunted, sad look in her eyes but some part of him saw hope in knowing that she missed him, too.

The days dragged on. A week became two. Then a month. By the end of the fourth month, Zane couldn't wait any longer. He needed to talk to her. He needed to look into her eyes and know if she was every bit as miserable as he was. He hadn't caught a glimpse of her for over a week and it was driving him crazy.

Four months was more than enough time to convince *him* that Celeste was the only woman he wanted to spend the rest of his life with, so maybe it was enough for her, too. If the only reason she wasn't calling was because he'd insisted on six months then they were both wasting valuable time apart that could be much better spent together.

Having made up his mind, Zane took a shower. He combed his now shoulder length hair, thinking that maybe he should have gone for a trim, but Celeste *had* really liked fisting her hands in it before. He took scissors to his beard and mustache, then shaved his face baby smooth, just like Celeste preferred. Then he pulled on his super-soft faded Levi's, the ones she told him he looked especially sexy in, and a dark blue, brushed cotton long sleeve T that strained across his chest and arms (he'd been working out a *lot* at the gym as an outlet in her absence).

Taking a deep breath, he stood outside her front door and rang the bell. While he waited, he imagined all sorts of scenarios. His favorite was the one where she opened the door, threw herself into his arms, and they made love for the rest of the night. That one was followed closely by his least favorite - the one where she opened the door, took one look at him, then thanked him for having the foresight to see they were going nowhere and closed the door in his face.

A minute passed, maybe two. He rang the bell again, wondering if maybe it was out again. So he knocked. Several times. No sound came from within; no music, no approaching footsteps, no warning bark.

Remembering the last time he was in a similar position, dread pooled in the pit of his stomach. Bradley was gone, but he wasn't the only psycho in the world. There were any number of sick bastards running loose, raping and murdering women. Suddenly the scenarios in his head took a decidedly dark and unwelcome turn.

He knew Celeste's security system. Knew it

because he had designed and installed it while she'd been in the hospital. Praying that she hadn't changed the access code, he punched in the number. He breathed a huge sigh of relief when the system disarmed. If nothing else, it demonstrated that she still had faith and trust in him.

Zane opened the door and stepped inside. "Celeste?" The call echoed strangely through the tiny foyer. Had she *still* not gotten any furniture?

"Celeste, it's Zane. Are you here?"

The answer became clear a moment later when he stepped into the living room. It was empty. Completely empty. Not a single box, computer screen, tablet or modem. Her banquet-sized folding table was gone, as was the rolling desk chair.

A quick inspection revealed the entire place was just as deserted. The kitchen was devoid of plates, pots, pans, and utensils. There were no towels, razor, or shampoo in the bathrooms, just a solitary roll of toilet paper in each. And in the bedroom, the place where he had found heaven so many times, there was not a trace of clothing; the spot on the floor where her mattress had been, bare.

Celeste was gone.

Zane stood in the center of the room and struggled to breathe, suddenly feeling like he had been sucked into a black hole. The moment he regained his sense of balance, he whipped out his cell phone.

"Where is she?" he demanded, hating the way

his voice echoed in the empty space. It felt too much like the inside of his chest.

Mitch's heavy sigh was easily heard over the mobile. "Her lease expired last month. She decided not to renew."

"You didn't think that was worth mentioning?"

"You didn't ask."

Zane felt like he'd taken a wrecking ball to the gut. "Is she safe?"

A pause. "Yes."

Zane ended the call, spewing a string of foul curses as he did so. He squeezed the small device in his hand hard, fighting the urge to throw it against the brick hearth. The only thing that kept him from doing so was the chance that Celeste might still try to call him in two more months when his deadline expired.

* * *

"So what do you think?" Celeste asked, her voice echoing in the vast empty space. "We did good, right?"

Jax sat beside her, panting softly. She reached down and gently scratched behind his ears. It was everything she'd ever wanted. A secluded beachfront property. A huge house built into the side of a mountain with an amazing view. Floor-to-ceiling windows looked out over the ocean below. Five bedrooms, six bathrooms, ten fireplaces. The kitchen alone was roughly the size of her first apartment. The residence also boasted a library, an on-site office, a home theater, and a small fitness room.

The place was absolutely stunning, but it was far too big for just the two of them.

As if he understood, the dog licked her hand. She would have been lost without Jax these past months. He had become her constant companion, her confidant, her protector, the furry shoulder she cried on when it all got to be too much. At first, she'd thought Zane had taken her to the animal shelter for the sole purpose of crossing yet another item off her bucket list. But now she saw the brilliance of his plan. He'd made sure that she wouldn't be alone when he wasn't there anymore.

Zane. Sweet, wonderful, stubborn man. He thought her feelings were based upon some romantic fairy tale. That because he had ridden in on his white horse and saved the day, she had been blinded by his heroic chivalry and felt compelled to say those three weighty words.

Well, it was partially true. Zane was her white knight; her modern day Prince Charming. But he was also the man she'd fallen in love with *before* James had come for her. The one who made her body sing, who made her laugh, and who took it upon himself to help her *live*.

Zane also thought that she should be far more upset over the chipping than she was. Granted, it did cross a serious personal boundary, and she would have preferred he discuss the idea with her first. If he had, she probably would have agreed to it right then and there anyway. She had known that when James did get out of prison, he wouldn't let a little thing like the law stop him, and that alone would have been enough reason to ensure that someone would always be able to find her. The truth was, she had no idea that kind of thing was even possible, but if she had, there was a good chance she would have done it herself.

And how could she fault him for that momentary lack of judgment when it had saved her life?

Four months ago, he'd walked away, telling her she needed the time and space to sort out her feelings. And if, at the end of six months, she still felt the same way, he would be waiting. No matter how many times she'd tried to tell him otherwise, he'd remained resolute, leading her to believe that *he* was the one who really needed the time and space to accept the truth.

Yet it was he who continually broke the terms of his own agreement. Oh, she'd seen him at the park, watching from afar. She'd sensed him nearby, even when he remained out of sight. Always there, always looking out for her. It affirmed what she already knew – that he did love her – and gave her hope that he would eventually figure it out.

Only two months to go, then she would know

for sure. Which didn't give her a lot of time to prepare. Thankfully, Mitch and her mother were behind her one hundred percent, because she was going to need both of them to make this work.

Chapter 16

"Zane. Did you hear what I said? CK wants a face-to-face."

Zane blinked, called back to the present by Mitch's irritated tone. "What?"

"CK? The owner of Cosmos Digital Solutions? The company that has agreed to pay all of your start-up costs and finance Fagan Home Security Systems? Does that ring a bell?"

"Can't you do it?" Zane rubbed the scruff on his jaw, turning the smart phone over and over in his other hand. All he had to do was activate the tracking app and within minutes he would know exactly where Celeste was. His six month deadline passed a week ago, and there had been no word from her.

Not a goddamn word. No phone call, no text, no frigging email. And she sure as hell hadn't shown up at his door and stepped into his empty frigging arms.

"Not this time," Mitch said firmly. "I've handled everything I can for you, Zane, but this is a deal-breaker. CK wants to speak with you personally or no funding."

"What the hell for? You've shown him the paperwork, laid out the bottom line. Nobody can beat my systems."

"Yes, and that has gotten your foot in the door, but CK's old fashioned; thinks the success of a business depends more on the person behind it than a bunch of numbers on paper." Mitch paused, looking at Zane, similar blue eyes pinning him with the force of a laser. "You really need to do this, Zane."

Zane tried to work up enough energy to care, but couldn't. He didn't care much about anything. Each day was a sorry repeat of the one before it: Get up. Work out. Try to work, but spend more time staring at his phone, alternating between willing it to ring and fighting the urge to activate the tracker. Assuming she hadn't had it removed, that was.

Eventually he'd accomplish something, enough to be able to call it a day. Then he'd drink a few beers and feel sorry for himself. Go to bed early and dream about Celeste until it was time to wake up and start the cycle all over again.

"Zane. You can't keep doing this to yourself. You have to move on."

Deep down, Zane knew Mitch was right, but there didn't seem to be much point, really. What did he have to look forward to? All the things he enjoyed before held little appeal for him now. He had no desire whatsoever to start going out again. There was only one woman he wanted to be with. Other things – like going sailing, riding his Harley, listening to music – all reminded him of *her*.

"Is that what Celeste did, Mitch? Move on?"

"You didn't give her any choice."

Yeah, Zane thought. *That's because I'm a fucking idiot.* Mitch had hit that nail right on the head. He still remembered the tears in her eyes when she asked him not to go, but he had been so scared that one day she would come to her senses and leave him, too. Everyone had tried to tell him he was making a mistake, but he hadn't listened. He was too much of a coward, being the first to walk away so that he wouldn't be hurt later.

Now he realized that he should have pulled her into his arms and taken every minute he could with her, loving her. He should have taken every opportunity to convince her that he was the only man for her. Now it was too late. By pushing her away he had ensured that what he feared most had come to pass. Talk about a self-fulfilling prophecy.

It took most of the evening, but Mitch was very persistent, and Zane finally agreed that he would meet with the CEO of Cosmos Digital Technologies.

Zane borrowed Mitch's Lexus for the drive. Knowing next to nothing about this mysterious CK

– Mitch was very tight-lipped about the guy, saying only that CK was a very private, reclusive sort – he wasn't sure how the Shelby or the Harley would come across. Mitch had been adamant that Zane's making a good impression was critical to his future.

Zane found it hard to care, but Mitch had put a lot of work into this deal, and he owed him this much at least. Mitch had put up with him for the last six months; had endured all of his moods, moping, and general lack of interest in the world around him.

That was how he found himself driving up the coast toward the GPS coordinates he'd been provided. At Mitch's insistence, he was once again clean and well-groomed. None of those things mattered when you didn't go anywhere or do anything. With Celeste gone, which all but eliminated the chance of running into her, he had stopped bothering.

The sun was out when he left, but the cloud cover thickened the farther he crawled up the coastline. By the time he exited the highway and navigated the increasingly smaller roads, it was downright gloomy. It matched his mood.

When he pulled into the drive and came across the house built right into the side of the mountain, even he had to appreciate the guy's style. It sat alone above the shoreline, miles away from the nearest town with no other houses in sight, surrounded by ancient, tall trees on the other sides. The place was built to blend in with the land around

it, varying offset levels of wood and stone,
reminding him of some of the architectural wonders
of Frank Lloyd Wright. Huge floor to ceiling panes
of tinted glass on each story looked out over the
ocean.

It was the type of place Celeste would have
loved.

Brutally shoving that thought to the back of his
mind, Zane got out of the car and stretched. The
ride had managed to eat up a few hours of his day.
Not that it mattered, really. It wasn't like he had
anything better to do. If nothing else, maybe this
CK guy would turn out to be interesting enough to
distract him for a little while.

Following the loosely cobbled walkway, Zane
made his way up to what he assumed was the proper
entrance and rang the bell before noticing the small
printed sign: *Bell doesn't work. Please come around
to back entrance.*

Yes, Zane thought with another stab of pain, he
could definitely envision Celeste here.

Zane turned the far corner of the building and
froze. A beautiful stone patio spread out before him,
complete with a fire pit currently boasting a
welcoming blaze. Comfortable looking and stylish
outdoor furniture flanked the pit. And sitting there,
with her back to him, was a woman who had hair
like sunlight and honey.

Like Celeste.

Zane swallowed, hard, then turned on his heel

and began to walk the other way. He couldn't do this. No fucking way. Even Fate couldn't be that cruel.

"Mr. Fagan." The voice called out before he could make it fully around the corner. Christ, it even sounded like Celeste. "Mr. Fagan, please wait."

He heard the padding of pawed feet and the rhythmic click of nails on stone only seconds before the low warning growl. He stopped, but didn't turn around. He couldn't.

"*Zane.*"

The touch upon his arm was whisper light. The scent familiar. It couldn't be.

"Celeste?"

He turned and looked down into the same liquid amber eyes that had been haunting his dreams. He searched her face for something – anything – that would explain this. Her skin was just as dewy and fresh as he remembered. Her hair was a bit longer, with perhaps more blonde streaks than had been there before. Beside her, a familiar furry face looked up at him.

"You're CK?" he said as the pieces started falling into place.

She offered a cautious smile. "Celeste Karliena Harrison."

Zane blinked, frozen to the spot. Then it began to dawn on him. *Celeste had called.* Celeste had requested a private meeting. With him. She had refused to meet with anyone but him.

"The CEO of Cosmos Digital Technologies."

She bit her bottom lip and flushed. "Pretty much the whole company, actually. It's getting to be a bit hard to manage. I thought it might be wise to consider a merger."

The damn of ice that had built itself in his chest since he'd walked away from her began to crack. "Did you now?" he asked softly.

Celeste cleared her throat. "Yes. Don't get me wrong. I *can* continue to go it alone but I would prefer not to."

A few leaks sprung. "Given it a lot of thought, have you?"

"I have done my research. You, Mr. Fagan, are exactly what I am looking for."

Huge blocks of ice dislodged and shattered into a thousand tiny pieces. "You are quite sure about that?"

"There is no doubt in my mind."

There was not a chance in hell he was going to wait another minute. She had her chance to walk away. He wasn't going to give her another opportunity. Ever.

He pulled Celeste into his arms and crushed her against his chest. Capturing her mouth with his, he claimed it. Completely. Totally. Brutally.

In a matter of seconds all of the familiar urges crashed into him like a tsunami, rolling over him and giving him no chance. Celeste's clothes were gone, as were his. A suspiciously convenient pile of blankets became a cozy little nest.

"I don't have a condom," he panted against her skin, desperate to taste every inch.

"I don't care," she said. "I need you, Zane. All of you."

There would be time for finesse and gentleness later, but they were way past any of that. Zane reached between her legs and found her wet and ready. Without another thought, he slid into her, nearly sobbing from the joy of it.

Her nails dug into his back as he pumped frantically, needing to brand her thoroughly before she had a chance to change her mind. Her hips rolled to meet him, deepening his penetration until every last inch was filled and aching with need.

"Celeste!" he cried out, bucking deep when he felt her squeezing around him in the grips of climax. He followed immediately, pumping his soul into her right along with his seed.

Hours later, Celeste sat in between Zane's legs, her back to his front, with the large blanket around both of them. It was only temporary; both knew and accepted that it wouldn't be long before they heeded the call once again. Below them, the waves swelled and crashed against the surf.

"I thought you wanted a cabin in the mountains."

"I did. But then I saw this place, and thought of you and how much you liked the ocean. Did I mention there's a private dock? I looked at a couple of sailboats, but I didn't know enough about them to choose wisely, so I asked Mitch to help me. I hope you like it."

Her words sank in. "You did this... for me?"

"Well, duh," she said softly. "A future without you wasn't an option, Zane."

He didn't know what to say. His chest felt like it was going to explode. After several long minutes, he cleared his throat and said. "Well. I guess I'll be signing those merger papers then, huh?"

"Only if you feel it's in your best interests," she said, her eyes glittering. "What did your legal counsel recommend?"

"Oh," Zane said, shifting them around so that she was beneath him. "He suggested a complete merging of assets."

He slid into her easily, her channel still slick from their previous lovemaking.

"Hmm," she hummed, welcoming him as she ran her nails up his back. "I do like the sound of that..."

Epilogue

Three Months Later

"Rrrmmphf."

Zane ignored Jax's soft plea and snuggled into the warm, fragrant woman in his arms.

"Rrrrmmphf." A cold, wet nose prodded insistently in the middle of his bare back.

Popping an eye open, the brilliant daylight flooding the room registered. He yawned and lifted his head to check the digital clock display. "Celeste, wake up, baby. We overslept."

She groaned and pulled the covers up over her head. Zane pulled them down again. "Come on, sexy genius. Mitch and your mother are going to be here soon. We've got to get ready."

Celeste's eyes popped open. "What time is it?"

"Nearly eleven."

"Crap." She sat up quickly, then promptly turned a sickly shade of green.

"Here." Zane reached beside the bed and grabbed the pack of saltines and a miniature-sized bottled water. "Settle our little guy while I take care of Jax." He punctuated his words by lovingly running a hand over the barely-there swell of her belly.

"I knew I made the right decision in agreeing to marry you."

He chuckled and pressed a kiss to her bare shoulder. "I thought it was because of my amazing rod."

"That amazing rod is why we overslept and will probably be late for our own wedding."

"Totally worth it," he said unrepentantly.

He reluctantly rolled away from his pregnant fiancé and business partner and found not one, but two pairs of soulful eyes – one brown, one blue - staring at him expectantly. Not long after Zane had moved in with Celeste, they'd made another trip to the animal shelter and let Jax pick out a companion. The dog had made a beeline towards the back, planting his haunches in front of a fluffy white Samoyed female, and Sammie became the newest member of their household.

Zane pulled on his jeans, looking over his shoulder when he felt Celeste's gaze. Sure enough, she was staring at his backside with blatant appreciation. And just like that, his blood warmed. Since her morning sickness had taken hold, wake-up sex was not on the agenda, but he wasn't complaining. The extended mid-day and late night sessions driven by Celeste's rampant hormones were *epic*.

"Like what you see?" he smirked.

"I do indeed."

"Maybe after I let these guys out, I'll come back and we can - "

"Have sex?" she finished, a hopeful gleam in her eye.

"I was going to say, shower together to save time, but I like the way you think."

"Maybe we can do both."

That idea certainly had its merits. Images of a wet, soapy Celeste had him hard and aching as he ushered their charges out of the bedroom before he gave in to his urges and climbed back into bed with her. He let them out into the large fenced-in area reserved for unsupervised outside time and started a pot of coffee. While he waited for that to brew, he toasted a couple of bagels and poured some juice, then arranged everything on a tray.

He leaned back against the counter and took a deep breath. In six months, he was going to be a father. In six hours, he would be a married man. Celeste already carried his child; by tonight she would wear his ring and bear his name as well.

By all accounts, he should have been freaking out, but as the gentle breeze carried in the muted sounds of the ocean and the ever-present squawks of gulls, he felt only peace. The wedding wasn't going to change anything, not really. He and Celeste were already joined in every way that mattered, personally and professionally.

He'd moved in right after their "meeting" three months earlier, unwilling to waste even one more precious moment with her. Since neither of them had much in the way of furniture, they'd spent the next few weeks picking out things and decorating the place together. The result was a home that they both loved, crafted more for comfort than style.

Their businesses had officially merged shortly thereafter and their joint venture – Cosmos Digital Security – was proving to be quite lucrative, indeed. With his knowledge of security and Celeste's mad computer skills, they'd developed unparalleled new systems for home and personal security. Not only were they receiving more orders every day, he got to make his own hours and work from his home office. They each had their own private space to facilitate getting anything done, because they'd discovered that being in the same room for any length of time could be too distracting.

One of the perks was that when either of them felt like taking a break, all they had to do was wander around until they found the other.

Best job ever.

In addition to being technologically brilliant, Celeste was loving and funny and, in his opinion, the perfect woman. He couldn't imagine his life without her. So no, he wasn't nervous at all. If anything, he couldn't wait to make it all official. In a few hours, Celeste Karliena Harrison would become Mrs. Zane Fagan and that sounded damn good to him.

A soft woof at the back door informed him that Jax and Sammie were ready to come back in. Zane obliged, scooped out some dog food and refilled the water dishes.

Celeste was in the shower when he entered the bedroom with the tray a few minutes later. He wasted no time in stripping out of his jeans and joining her.

"Yes? Can I help you?" she teased when he slid in behind her.

He grabbed the body wash and the soft poof and began to wash her back. "Shower sex? Sound familiar?"

"Hmmm. Vaguely. Maybe you could refresh my memory."

Zane abandoned the poof, gliding his large hands along her curves. She leaned back into him, nestling his now-raging erection against the soft swells of her backside. He groaned when his palms reached her fuller breasts, the hardened tips prominently begging for attention.

"You are so fucking hot," he breathed. "How did I get so lucky?"

Celeste turned, taking him in her hand. "I think I'm the lucky one," she said. Her once tentative touch was now bold, confident. *Perfect.*

"I think we can agree that we're both – *Celeste!*"

She'd slipped through his hands and gone down

on her knees. He tangled his fingers in her hair and fought the urge to buck his hips as she loved him with that skilled, sassy mouth. Celeste targeted every one of his weaknesses mercilessly and before long he was ready to explode. With one smooth move, he cupped her beneath the arms, turning her around as he lifted her up. Her hands flattened against the tile and he slid into her warm, welcoming depths.

"Christ, I love you, Celeste." Zane reached around and used his fingers to hasten her pleasure; he was far too close for a slow, proper build-up. Thankfully he, like her, had been paying attention and knew exactly where to stroke and squeeze to get her to her peak quickly. She tensed and gripped him hard, pushing them both over the edge.

"Thanks," she panted softly. "I needed that."

"My pleasure," he chuckled. Zane kissed her on the nose. "Think that will be enough to hold us till tonight?"

"Probably not. But there's got to be storage closet or hidden alcove somewhere, right?" she grinned.

"Naughty girl." He landed a soft tap on her backside. "Now let's move. The sooner we say I do, the sooner you're mine."

Celeste slid her arms up around his neck. "I'm already yours. Don't you know that?"

"Yes. But let's do this anyway."

* * *

It was hard to refrain from running the length of the small chapel. Zane looked so handsome in his black tux, standing before the altar; her heart fluttered against the walls of her chest at the very sight of him. She loved him so much, and soon they would officially be husband and wife.

Celeste followed behind her mother as the wedding march played softly in the background. Mitch walked her down the aisle, then took his place next to Zane. She laughed when she saw Jax already there, sporting a white silk collar and black bow tie. Facing him was Sammie, wearing a rhinestone collar draped in a glittering, soft tulle to make it look like a veil.

"Thought we'd make it a double wedding," Zane murmured with a wink.

Celeste handed her bouquet to her mother, whose eyes shone with unshed moisture, then turned to Zane.

"Shall we begin?" asked the minister.

She took a deep breath and nodded. Zane did the same.

"Dearly beloved, we are gathered here today…"

Before she knew it, Zane slid the ring onto her finger and they were pronounced man and wife. When he leaned in and kissed her for the first time as her husband, her toes literally curled. And she knew, without a doubt, that their happily ever after was just beginning…

A Note from Abbie

This is a work of fiction, but domestic violence is a very real problem. According to www.safehorizon.org:

- 25% of women will experience some form of domestic violence in their lifetimes. And attacks on men account for nearly 3 million assaults in the US.
- Domestic violence is a leading cause of homelessness.
- Children who witness domestic violence are more likely to be susceptible to abuse as adults, or become abusers themselves.
- Domestic violence costs run upwards of $37 billion per year in combined legal, medical, and law enforcement costs.

If you or someone you know is the victim of domestic violence, there is help available. Visit www.safehorizon.org or any one of many available sites for more information.

Thanks for reading Zane and Celeste's story

If you liked this book, then please consider posting a review online! It's really easy, only takes a few minutes, and makes a huge difference to independent authors who don't have the mega-budgets of the big-time publishers behind them.

Log on to Amazon (or Goodreads) and just tell others what you thought, even if it's just a line or two. That's it! A good review is one of the nicest things you can do for any author.

As always, I welcome feedback. Email me at abbiezandersromance@gmail.com. Or sign up for my mailing list on my website at http://www.abbiezandersromance.com for up to date info and advance notices on new releases, Like my FB page (AbbieZandersRomance), and/or follow me on Twitter (@AbbieZanders).

Thanks again, and may all of your ever-afters be happy ones!

♥ *Abbie*

Like short romantic comedies...

… with strong female heroines and former military heroes? Check out this excerpt from *The Realist*…

"Earth to Rissa." Travis' deep voice rolled through me like a wave, tugging me away from my reflections. His shortened address felt warm, intimate. No one had ever called me that before. "If you're finished ogling me, I'm going to head back to my place."

I felt the heat rise in my face. Yes, I had been ogling him, but I'd zoned out for the last couple of minutes. I don't know what bothered me more – the fact that he'd caught me in the act or that I'd wasted several minutes of prime ogling time.

"I'm done," I said casually, waving my hand in a shooing gesture. "You can go now."

He grinned cockily. "Lasagne."

"What?"

"That's what I want for dinner. Lasagne. With lots of meat and that chunky homemade sauce of yours."

I blinked, looking at him blankly.

"Our deal," he reminded me. "You get manual labor. I get food. Your roof is fixed. And I'm hungry for lasagne."

"Right," I nodded. I knew that. I did.

He leaned down and petted Ripper, the mangy stray who had become my shadow. The scent of clean male sweat and heat-activated deodorant tickled my nose and I discreetly filled my lungs with it.

"I'll be back around sundown. And Rissa?"

"Yeah?"

"Don't stare at my ass while I'm walking away. It's objectifying."

I openly gaped at him, but he just winked and strutted – yes, strutted – out of my kitchen like a big male peacock.

I showed him, though. I stared at his ass the whole way.

The Realist is available on Amazon now! Get your copy today.

Also by Abbie Zanders

Contemporary Romance

- 📖 Dangerous Secrets (Callaghan Brothers #1)
- 📖 First and Only (Callaghan Brothers #2)
- 📖 House Calls (Callaghan Brothers #3)
- 📖 Seeking Vengeance (Callaghan Brothers #4)
- 📖 Guardian Angel (Callaghan Brothers #5)
- 📖 Beyond Affection (Callaghan Brothers #6)
- 📖 Having Faith (Callaghan Brothers #7)
- 📖 Bottom Line (Callaghan Brothers #8)
- 📖 Five Minute Man (Covendale Series #1)
- 📖 All Night Woman (Covendale Series #2)
- 📖 The Realist

Time Travel Romance

- 📖 Lost in Time I
- 📖 Lost in Time II

Paranormal

- 📖 Vampire, Unaware
- 📖 Black Wolfe's Mate (writing as Avelyn McCrae)

About the Author

Abbie Zanders loves to read and write romance in all forms; she is quite obsessive, really. Her ultimate fantasy is to spend all of her free time doing both, preferably in a secluded mountain cabin overlooking a pristine lake, though a private beach on a lush tropical island works, too. Sharing her work with others of similar mind is a dream come true. She promises her readers two things: no cliffhangers, and there will always be a happy ending. Beyond that, you never know…